The King Bear

The King Bear

BY MICHAEL TURNER

Illustrated by Robert Frankenberg

GOLDEN PRESS ⮞ NEW YORK

To Jessie, my wife,
who shared with me
the vast, lonely beauty
of Alaska

Contents

THE BEAR 9

EYES IN THE NIGHT 15

NEARER TO EAGLES 33

TRAPPED 46

RESCUE 63

MAGIC YELLOW WINGS 79

THE CALF 94

TO BURY A MOOSE 108

AMBUSH AT THE CABIN 129

THE THUNDER OF RIFLES 146

A CLICKING, CLINKING, CLANKING 164

CHAPTER ONE

The Bear

BLUE-JOHN was hoeing the potato patch on his stepdad's Alaska homestead the first time he saw the bear. The bear walked out of the thick spruce and birch forest that stood like a great, green wall around most of his stepdad's farm. When the bear saw Blue-John it stopped. It stood and looked at the boy. Its golden-brown fur was a sharp contrast against the green darkness of the forest.

It was a very big bear.

Blue-John looked at the bear. It was not a black bear. He knew this from its broad head and the hump on its shoulders. And from its size. Black bears were sometimes brown in color. But never did a blackie grow as big as this bear!

The boy was young, and small, standing there alone in the potato patch in the Alaska bush country. In the setting sun, the tall, thin spruce trees threw long shadows onto the potato patch. The bear stood in one of these shadows, looking at the small boy.

Blue-John did not move. He knew he could not outrun the bear. The hoe felt like a thin little stick in his hand. He tried to swallow and couldn't. His mouth was suddenly very dry. He watched the bear.

Suddenly the bear moved. As if he had made up his mind, the big brown bear started into the potato patch. With the smooth, rolling, pigeon-toed way of a bear, he came walking slowly down a potato row. He was five rows away from Blue-John. He looked straight ahead, walking straight down the row. His great body swung from side to side, and his cinnamon-colored fur rippled smoothly over the massive muscles underneath.

He walked pigeon-toed right past Blue-John without even looking at him, and went on down the row. Blue-John's feet were like roots in the loose clay soil. He thought that even if the bear had been in his row, he could not have gotten out of the way. The bear would have had to walk over him, he thought.

Blue-John had seen black bears in the vast miles of forest around the homestead. While hunting moose with his stepdad he had watched blackies licking up blueberries or digging out mice. His stepdad had shot one that had raided their rabbit hutches one late fall night. The bear had easily torn apart the wire-and-wood cages, and had plucked out a fat, white doe. The bear had sat down to eat the rabbit, then and there. His stepdad, aiming by moonlight, had shot the bear stone dead, then and there.

This bear was not like that one.

This bear was a grizzly.

"He walks like a king," said Blue-John to himself, swiveling his head to stare after the bear. "He acts just like he owns this old spud patch, and the woods . . . and the whole homestead. . . ."

The great bear strolled out of the potato patch and crossed a band of red fireweed. He went into the forest.

"A king!" thought Blue-John. "A bygolly king!"

For a moment the small boy stood, still as a post, staring after the bear. A great horned owl hooted from the dark, quiet forest. Blue-John jumped at the sound. Then, suddenly, his knees were weak. His legs began shaking. He felt chilly all over. He sat down.

He just sat for a while, a boy with straw-colored hair, in faded jeans, among the green potatoes. He thought about the bear. For a moment he thought maybe he hadn't really seen it. It had been so big, so close, it couldn't have been real. It hadn't made a sound. It had just lumbered past, silent as a shadow.

No! The bear *had* made a sound. Suddenly Blue-John remembered the steady, soft thudding of the animal's feet as it came down the row he had hoed this morning.

Blue-John jumped up and ran across the rows, searching the ground. In the fifth row over he found what he was looking for.

Footprints.

There, in the newly hoed clay, were the tracks left by the bear. Blue-John stepped into a track. He put both of his boots side by side inside one broad footprint. He stepped to the next footprint and did the same thing.

He looked up and down the row, tracing with his eyes the trail of bold, broad tracks.

"Looks like he tracked up the potato patch just to show he didn't care who knowed he was here," whispered Blue-John.

He went back to work, chopping out weeds. Now and then he glanced at the woods where the big bear had gone. The sun went down in a red sky behind the dark forest. Then the red sky faded to gray. The forest became darker.

Suddenly a dog barked, shattering the stillness. Blue-John looked toward his home, across the potato patch and the big vegetable garden. His mother had just thrown kitchen scraps to their flock of chickens.

"Probably potato and carrot peelings," thought the boy. "Stew tonight."

A small, woolly, brown and white dog was teasing a big rooster. It was Burrs, Blue-John's dog. The dog would charge the rooster, barking fiercely and stopping just short of the big bird. The rooster would dance away from the dog and circle back to the flock of chickens, who were fussing over the kitchen scraps. The little dog, barking and yapping, would charge the rooster again, getting closer each time.

Blue-John watched. "Burrs," he whispered, "you're sure gonna get it." Suddenly there was a flash of white wings as the big bird sprang head on to meet the charging dog. The rooster hooked Burrs in the muzzle with both spurs.

Burrs screamed with pain and surprise and flipped over backwards, scrambling to escape the rooster. Yowling and howling, the dog raced for the house.

"Burrs," groaned Blue-John, "when are you ever going to learn about roosters?"

The rooster shook himself, then poked a few feathers back into place. Stretching his neck and throwing out his chest, he crowed loud and long. Then he strutted proudly back to the flock.

Blue-John's mother went back into the house. In a moment a light winked on in the kitchen, flickered, and went out. It came on again, and stayed on.

Blue-John shouldered his hoe and walked, bobbing, across fourteen rows of potatoes. He crossed the vegetable garden, with its lettuce, cabbages, carrots, turnips, and pyramids of strawberries. He thought of the countless weeds he had hacked to shreds here.

He vaulted over a snow fence built of rough boards and walked toward the barn. From inside the fenced barnyard a fat, black and white cow watched him. He stopped, ripped up a handful of wild grass and offered it to the cow through the fence rails. The cow just stood there, calmly chewing her cud.

Blue-John tossed the grass into the barnyard. "Better eat up, Molly. You got that calf coming pretty soon, now. My calf!"

He went on to the toolshed to put away his hoe. The toolshed was small and built of rough boards. It seemed to lean against the big log barn as if it were tired. The toolshed door was always open. One hinge was broken. As he passed the toolshed, Blue-John tossed the hoe in the open door. It clattered among the other tools.

CHAPTER TWO

Eyes in the Night

H E crossed the yard of native grass between the toolshed and the house. In the middle of the yard was the well, with a small, square wooden platform covering the mouth of the well. A long-handled pump stood on the platform, with a tin dipper hanging from it.

Blue-John stopped at the well. He unhooked the battered dipper and held it under the pump spout. The pump squeaked and squawked as he swung the handle up and down. Half a dozen strokes with the handle and water gushed from the spout. He filled the dipper, tipped it up, and took a long drink of the cold, clear water. He flipped some water at the big white rooster still strutting in the yard, hung up the dipper, and continued on toward the house. On

15

the way he scattered the chickens, snatched up some potato peelings, and stuck them in a shirt pocket.

The screen door banged and bounced and banged again as he bounded into the kitchen.

"Hi, Mom, it's me," he announced.

"I thought for sure it was a bull moose," replied his mother. She had lit gas lanterns in the kitchen and living room. Now she was working at the kitchen counter, shaping a big lump of soft, white dough.

"Biscuits?" asked Blue-John.

"Biscuits," answered his mother, dropping the dough into the middle of a patch of flour spread on the counter. She got a rolling pin from a drawer and started to roll out the dough.

Blue-John's mother was not a very tall woman, and she was a little plump. Her hair was light brown, slightly gray, and usually mussed. Smile wrinkles made a net of tiny lines at the corners of her eyes.

She started punching out disks of dough with a glass.

Blue-John got two soda crackers from a box in the cabinet and stuck them in his pocket. He got a leaf of lettuce and some scraps of moosemeat from the refrigerator and went into his bedroom. Along one wall, on a high bench, were three homemade wire cages. In one cage were three meadow mice. He gave them a cracker, half the lettuce, and a handful of oat kernels from a tin can under the bench. He went to the second cage. In it a parka squirrel jumped up the cage wall to greet him. He gave the squirrel the remaining cracker and lettuce, the potato peelings from the yard, and a handful of cornflakes. The squirrel raced around the cage. Finally, into the third cage he dropped the little chunks of moosemeat. Using a tin can he got water from the bathroom for all the animals. As he left the room a small owl dropped to the floor of the third cage, picked up a piece of meat, and hopped back up on its perch to eat. Blue-John went back to the kitchen.

He sniffed the big iron kettle on the stove. "Mmm," he said. "Moose stew."

"Uh huh," replied his mother. She dropped the disks of dough into a pan and put the pan in the oven. "We're about out of moosemeat. I'm glad this is August. You and your dad will have to go out and shoot a moose one of these days."

Blue-John said, "Yeah. Hey, Mom! I seen a bear!"

His mother was cleaning the kitchen counter. "Blueberries should be about ripe, too," she said. "We're all out of them. All out."

"He was brown, and big as a truck," Blue-John went on, getting excited as he talked about the bear.

"Need cranberries, too," continued his mother. "Seems we always eat more than we pick."

Blue-John was following his mother around the kitchen. "He—he walked right past me." He held out his arms. "This close!"

His mother started to set the table. "How many potatoes did you get hoed, honey?"

"Mom!" cried the boy. "You ain't listening! It was a grizzly. In the dumb old potato patch. This close! Look!"

"Sure, my brave son. You saw a bear, this close." She smiled and spread apart her thumb and forefinger. "I sure wish your dad would get home and start the generator, so we could have some electricity. These gas lanterns are all right for light but they won't run my eggbeater."

"Aw, Mom, you just don't LISTEN to me!" Blue-John said.

He went out on the porch. He sat down on the step and put his chin in his hands. He gazed out across the south yard, toward the hayfield.

The screen door banged. Burrs burst onto the porch and leaped upon Blue-John. The little dog wiggled and squirmed, licking the boy's face. Blue-John's younger stepsister, Angie, came out and sat down beside him.

"Betcha don't know what I made today," she said. Like Blue-John, she was wearing blue denims. She dragged a big red woman's purse behind her. A woman's hat made of bright blue feathers hung loosely over one eye. Her short, blond hair stuck out from under the hat.

Blue-John didn't answer.

"Well," his sister went on, "I'll tell you about it, so's you can guess."

Blue-John played with Burrs.

Angie got a half-eaten carrot from her purse, bit off a piece, and put the carrot back in her purse. "I made it from a old box. In my room. Come on, Blue-John, guess!"

"Go away, huh?" answered her stepbrother.

"I made it all purple-green with crayon. It's got a door and everything. You can come see it if you want." She smiled. "Want some carrot?"

"Aw, just leave me alone, will you?" He watched Burrs prance into the yard to challenge the white rooster.

"Gee, you're a sourpuss! I just wanted to show you my playhouse, is all." Angie got up to leave.

"Well, I ain't going to look at your old girl's playhouse. Besides"—he turned to look across the distant potato patch—"Besides, I got something better."

"I bet! I just bet!" said Angie, going into the house. "Well, I just won't give you no carrot, either."

Blue-John watched the hayfield. He stood up as a steady snarl grew louder from the direction of the hayfield. Coming across the hayfield was his stepdad, driving a tractor. The sound of the tractor gradually surged louder and closer. His stepdad drove into the barn lot between the barn and the tractor shed and bounced to a stop. He shut off the engine and slowly climbed down from the high tractor seat. He walked toward the house, limping. At the pump on the well he stopped for a drink.

"Ahh," he said, as he hung up the dipper. "Now, that's water. Hi, John." He came up on the porch. "Did you chop out all the spuds and leave the weeds?" He patted Blue-John on the shoulder and went into the kitchen.

Blue-John followed. "Dad, guess what I saw in . . ." he started to say.

"Hi, wife," said his stepdad.

"Hi, Mr. Brinkman," said Blue-John's mother, smiling. "Want a cup of coffee?"

Mr. Brinkman hung his cap on a rack near the door. "You bet!" He sniffed the pan of moose stew on the stove. "Mmmm."

"Dad," said Blue-John.

Mr. Brinkman carried his cup of coffee into the living room and began walking slowly back and forth. Blue-John watched his stepdad.

"Leg hurt?" he asked.

"A little," answered Mr. Brinkman. "I guess I never

will get over that bulldozer accident." He stretched his right leg and rubbed it. "Have to loosen it up a little. Got that hoe worn out yet?" He grinned at the boy.

"It's wearing me out, I guess," answered Blue-John. "Dad, if I tell you something, you gotta promise to listen, okay?"

"Sure," replied Mr. Brinkman, still walking. "I promise." He put his coffee on a table and rubbed his leg with both hands.

Blue-John stepped directly in front of his stepdad and put his hands on his hips. "Dad. You'll never guess what I saw today. Out in the potato patch. Just guess what I seen!"

His stepdad grinned. "Why, a grizzly bear, of course." He winked at Blue-John.

Blue-John stared at his stepdad. "How did you know?"

"Know what?"

"How did you know I seen a . . ." Blue-John started to say, then stopped. He realized his stepdad was teasing.

"Aw, Dad, you was just foolin'!" cried the boy. "I mean really! I sure enough seen a . . ."

"Will," Mrs. Brinkman called. "Would you start the generator? I need some electricity."

"Okay, Christine. Right away." He finished his

coffee with a gulp. "Come on, John. Help me start
the light-maker."

Blue-John followed his stepfather through the
kitchen and outside to a small lean-to room attached
to the kitchen. The lean-to was strongly built of rough
boards, with a door that latched. Mr. Brinkman went
inside and Blue-John followed.

In the lean-to was a diesel engine and, next to it,
an electric generator. The engine ran the generator,
and the generator made electricity for the homestead. Electric lights weren't needed during the day
and the machines were shut off. The refrigerator,
freezer, and the kitchen stove were run by gas that
came in big steel bottles. The big bottles stood in a
row outside the kitchen.

Mr. Brinkman started the diesel engine. It roared
to life, and the small room seemed to tremble with
the sound.

Mr. Brinkman pulled a lever connecting the engine
to the generator. The generator started. An electric
light came on in the generator room. A light on a
tall pole near the tractor shed suddenly bathed the
darkening yard with light. In the house, electric lights
filled the rooms with warm yellow light. Mr. Brinkman made an adjustment to the engine and the roar
settled to a purr.

"Okay, Blue-John, my boy," he said, clapping the

boy on the shoulder, "now we're civilized."

As they were going in the house Mr. Brinkman said, "One of these days the whole Kenai Peninsula will have electric power, and we won't need this home generator."

The sound of the engine, locked up and muffled in the small room, was a small, soft, steady purr in the twilight.

"Supper will be ready soon as I whip up these potatoes," announced Mrs. Brinkman.

Mr. Brinkman went into the bathroom to wash. Blue-John followed him. Angie followed Blue-John. Mr. Brinkman poured water from a big tin pitcher into the basin.

"Come see my playhouse," Angie said.

"Dad, Dad," began Blue-John. "I really seen it!"

"Saw, John, you *saw,*" said Mr. Brinkman, soaping his arms. "Saw what, the playhouse?"

"Aw, Dad, no! A bear!" cried Blue-John.

"It's purply-green, and has a chimbly," interrupted Angie.

"Oh, a purply-green bear with a chimney," said Mr. Brinkman. "Hmmm. You just don't find many of them." He rinsed off the soap and reached for a towel.

"No, Dad, that's not right," cried Blue-John, scowling at Angie.

23

"Sure isn't," answered Mr. Brinkman. "Bears don't have chimneys, do they?" He stepped out of the bathroom. Angie grabbed his hand.

"Come see it," she said.

"The bear?"

"I can show you the bear's tracks," said the boy, grabbing his stepdad's arm.

"Bear tracks in the playhouse?" Mr. Brinkman grinned. "Think I'll just stay out of that playhouse. And a purply-green bear." He shook his head. "Wash your hands, now, kids, and let's eat supper." He went to the kitchen, leaving Angie and Blue-John glaring at each other.

During supper Blue-John ate in silence. When supper was nearly finished Mr. Brinkman said, "You must be tired, John. You haven't said much tonight. I'll sharpen your hoe after supper, so you won't have to chop so hard."

"Aw, no, I ain't really much tired. Well—a little, maybe."

"Why so quiet, then?"

"Well—well, nobody believes I really saw a bear."

Mr. Brinkman was surprised. "You saw a bear? So that's what you and Angie were all steamed up about! You really did see a bear!"

"I sure did! And how I did!" said Blue-John, excited.

"Where?" asked his stepfather.

"Down in the potato patch. Today. This afternoon!"

Mr. Brinkman leaned back in his chair. "Hm!" he said. "We haven't had a bear come out of the woods since last summer."

Mrs. Brinkman asked, "Where did you see it? In the edge of the woods?"

"Heck no!" cried the boy. "That old bear just paraded down the potato patch like he owned it. Right past me!"

Mrs. Brinkman had started to get up for more coffee. Suddenly she sat down and stared at Blue-John. Mr. Brinkman leaned forward. Angie listened, openmouthed. "Right—past you?" asked his mother.

"I could hear his big feet hitting the ground as he went past," declared Blue-John.

"Well," said his stepfather. "That blackie is either stone blind or lazy as a toad. They usually avoid people like poison."

"Wasn't no black bear, said Blue-John, jumping to his feet. "This was a GRIZZLY!"

His mother gasped. "Now John, just sit down, and don't get so excited. You mean it was brown, not black?"

"Yeah! And big as a barn!"

"A brown black bear," said his father. "This one's probably old enough to be cranky and mean."

"No, Dad, no siree! It was a grizzly. I know!" Blue-John smiled, and sat down.

His stepfather smiled back. "Well, it looked like a brownie. A grizzly. Probably an overgrown brown blackie. Being big made it bold. I'll carry a rifle from now on. Might get a shot at it. And if you see it again, John, you get out of that potato patch quick, and get in the house. It's not afraid of people, and dangerous."

"Dad!" cried Blue-John. "Aw—heck!"

His mother said, "We're thankful the bear didn't jump you, son, but nobody's seen a grizzly around here for years. They're all up in the hills."

"Well, there's one down here, on this old farm, in the potato patch, and I seen it!"

As he talked, Blue-John's voice got louder, and higher, and finally he stood up, pointing across the kitchen toward the potato patch.

His stepfather put his hand on Blue-John's arm. "Tell you what, John. There's a difference between the footprints of a black and a grizzly. Now, this bear of yours. He must have made some prints, didn't he? Some tracks? In the dirt?"

"He sure did!" beamed Blue-John. "Oh boy, did he make some tracks for sure! All the way across the potato patch and into the woods!"

"Well, John, a brownie lays down tracks that look

like a black bear's except for two things. One is, the grizzly track is a lot bigger, of course. You might could get both feet in one, almost."

Blue-John nodded.

His stepdad poured himself some coffee. "And, a brownie prints his claws wherever he goes. His footprints have claw marks. A black bear's tracks don't have claw marks. Now, tomorrow morning we'll go down to the spud patch, first thing, and have a look at those tracks, and we'll know."

"But Dad, I already know. I stood in one of the tracks. With both feet."

Mr. Brinkman looked at Blue-John sideways and grinned. "And your feet didn't stick over the edges a little? Hmmm?"

"No. Honest, Dad."

"Were there claw marks?"

Blue-John hesitated. "Well, I—I don't remember. There might have been. Uh, can't we go tonight? Now?"

"Oh, John, it's too late tonight. First thing tomorrow, we'll go look."

Later that evening, Blue-John was in his room, when Angie came in.

"Whatcha doing?" she asked.

"Toasting marshmallows with a crocodile."

"Oh, John, you are *not*! You've got a maganet."

27

"Well, if you knew, why ask a dumb question?" asked Blue-John.

Angie sat down. "Can I play with the maganet?"

"In a minute, maybe." He lined up a dozen small nails, end to end. He touched the magnet to the end nail and lifted the first four nails.

Angie looked closely. "What sticks them together, glue?"

"Naw. Magnetism."

"Is maganetism some kind of glue?"

"Course not! It's—uh, it's—well, it's—magic."

"Gee!"

"I thought just about everybody knew that," said Blue-John. He shook the nails off the magnet, then he got up and closed the door.

"Hey!" he whispered. "Want to see some bear tracks?"

"Bear tracks? From a real bear?" asked Angie, her eyes wide.

"Well, sure a *real* bear! What'd you think, a teddy bear, or Winnie the Pooh?"

"Who's Wendy the Poo?"

"Oh, never mind," said Blue-John. "Forget I said it. Anyhow, let's go see my bear tracks, huh?"

"Tonight?"

"Sure. Tonight. Now. And don't talk so loud."

Angie peered over her shoulder at the darkness

outside the window. She hunched down beside Blue-John and whispered, "It's dark!"

"We'll take my flashlight. It works pretty good."

"And a lantern?" asked Angie.

"I don't know how to light it. 'Sides, a flashlight will do. We'll just go to the potato patch."

"That's a long way! And there's *things* out there, with big teeths, and—claws, and—big eyes!"

"Aw, rats. Ain't nothing to really hurt you," sneered Blue-John. "But I guess I should have knowed a little kid would be too scared to go out in the dark."

"Well, why don't you go your own self, smarty," asked Angie.

Blue-John pretended not to hear. He started picking up nails again with the magnet.

" 'Course," he said, "if you don't really want me to look at your dumb old playhouse, why, okay."

"Well, gee—*really*? Will you play in my playhouse when we get back?"

"Sure."

"With my Suzie doll?"

"Uh, yeah, I guess."

"And we'll have a tea party?"

"Aw, migosh! OKAY!"

Angie frowned. "What if the bear is there?" She leaned close to her stepbrother and whispered, "Will you make the bear not hurt us?"

"Sure."

Angie suddenly hugged Blue-John. "Oh, John, you are the goodest brother I ever had!"

Blue-John jumped to his feet. "Aw, for crying out loud! Let's just go, huh? I'll get my flashlight."

They went out casually past Mr. Brinkman, who was reading in the living room. In the kitchen Mrs. Brinkman glanced at them. "Going somewhere, kids?"

"Uh huh," answered Blue-John. "Be right back."

The two children trooped out of the kitchen and into the floodlit yard. The night was filled with the soft, steady purr of the diesel engine. They stood for a moment, two small figures in the yellow light.

Then, like two elves, they walked softly toward the velvety edge of the darkness. Their long, shapeless shadows bobbed ahead of them, and touched the darkness.

When they reached the darkness, Angie stopped.

"John." Her tiny voice was a whisper in the night. "John. I'm scared. What if the bear is there?"

"Aw, migosh. There ain't no bear."

"Is the potato place far?"

"Naw. Just out there." He pointed into the darkness.

"It's darker than it was in the house," she said.

Blue-John hesitated. He looked around. "It sure is."

"John, hold my hand."

"Okay." Blue-John took her hand. With his other hand he drew a flashlight from under his shirt and turned it on. He had to shake it to make it work. Its dim light didn't reach very far into the darkness.

Hand in hand, they slowly walked into the night, guided by the beam of the flashlight.

A horned owl hooted in the forest. It sounded sad, and lonely.

There was no moon. The stars were hidden by clouds.

Far away, a dog barked, twice, three times.

The children crossed rows of carrots, then cabbages, then turnips.

Finally they were stumbling over rows of potatoes.

"I'm cold," whispered Angie.

"We're almost there," answered Blue-John.

Suddenly he stopped, and searched the ground with the dim light from the flashlight. The flashlight went out and he shook it to make it work.

"Here!" he whispered hoarsely. "Here's the tracks! Right here is where he was!" He bent down to look at the great footprints.

Angie stood close to him, looking into the darkness, where the distant forest made a black wall of shadow against the dark sky.

"John," she whispered.

31

Blue-John was staring at the footprints.

"John, I heard something."

He whistled softly. "Look at those claw marks!"

He swung his flashlight to examine another footprint. For an instant the light swept across the potato patch, and the woods.

Angie gasped and clutched his shoulder. Her small voice trembled. "John—there's something out there."

He was still looking at tracks. "It *was* a grizzly!" He looked up. "Angie, what's the matter?"

She pointed into the darkness. "Over there."

Blue-John stood up and aimed the light where she pointed. At the end of the beam of light, two orange-red eyes watched them, staring out of the darkness.

Then, the flashlight went out.

Suddenly Blue-John and Angie were running, hand-in-hand, back through the darkness, across the potatoes, and the turnips, and the cabbages, and the carrots.

Angie stumbled on the rough ground, and fell, pulling Blue-John down with her. He helped her to her feet.

Behind them, a deep, rumbling growl echoed through the darkness.

CHAPTER THREE

Nearer to Eagles

ANGIE and Blue-John came running out of the darkness. When they reached the floodlit yard Angie fell again. Her stepbrother again helped her to her feet and they scrambled up the porch steps. They burst into the kitchen, breathless, and slammed the door.

"Angie! John!" cried their mother. "What's the matter? Where have you been?"

"Bear! Bear!" cried Angie, running to hide behind her mother. "Out there! Mama! Mama! It's really there! Big black gobble-you-up bear! Red eyes! Oh, Mama!" She clutched her mother.

Mr. Brinkman came running from the living room. "What bear? Where? John, where have you been?"

Blue-John suddenly felt very foolish at having risked Angie's life, and his own. He avoided looking

33

at his stepfather. He sat down, weak and trembly. "Out—out in the—spud patch," he muttered.

"What for!" thundered his stepfather.

Blue-John's voice croaked. "To—see the tracks of . . ." the words came out squeaky and hard to hear, ". . . the bear."

Mr. Brinkman shook his head. "Oh, John, ain't you got any *sense*? You told us forty times this evening that you had seen a bear out there and you go *right back* in the *dark* to where you had seen it, and take this little girl along, and risk both your necks just to look at its tracks, and it was *there* and and boy you're lucky you ain't standing there DEAD!" Mr. Brinkman was out of breath.

He turned to Angie. "It was a black bear, you say? It was that close?"

"Uh, Pop," John spoke up. "It wasn't close enough to see it. We just seen its eyes with the flashlight."

Mr. Brinkman thought for a moment, and then asked Blue-John, "Do you think it was the bear you saw this afternoon?"

"Might have been. Probably."

"Did you get a look at the tracks?"

"Sure did," answered Blue-John, glad to change the subject.

"Did they have claw marks?"

"Sure did."

Mr. Brinkman went to the door.

"Will, where are you going?" asked his wife.

"To run Molly and Ginger into the barn and close the door. It's not likely the bear would bother them but I'll just lock them up anyway." He put on his cap.

"Will, take a rifle," said Mrs. Brinkman.

"Just to go to the barn?" laughed her husband, and he went out.

"Your stepdad's as stubborn as you are, John," said Mrs. Brinkman as she picked up Angie. "Now, it's time for you kids to go to bed." She squeezed Angie. "Going to dream about bears, little scout?"

Angie shivered and hugged her mother. "No! Just puppy dogs!"

*   *   *

The next morning was bright and clear. The yellow sun scoured the shadows out of the deep forest and washed the homestead in warm sunlight. Field mice scurried through the tall native grass, looking for breakfast. A big raven stood in one of the bear's tracks.

At the homestead, the diesel engine was quiet. It had been shut off for the day.

Mrs. Brinkman hummed softly to herself in the kitchen as she prepared breakfast.

Blue-John and Angie came into the kitchen. They

were unusually quiet as they sat down at the table.

Mrs. Brinkman looked at each of them in turn and went on frying eggs. After a moment she said, "Morning, kittens."

"Hi, Mom," said Blue-John.

"Hi, Mom," said Angie.

They sat in silence.

Mr. Brinkman came in from the barn with a bucket of warm, foamy milk. He glanced at the children. "Hi, bear hunters," he said. He put the bucket on the floor next to a big, two-handled metal milk can. After fitting a big funnel into the top of the can, he got two round, white, thin, cotton filters out of a box and fastened them into the bottom of the funnel. He poured the milk into the funnel. The milk, cleansed of tiny bits of dirt and dust by the filters, dripped like a small waterfall into the can.

Mrs. Brinkman said, "Too bad Ginger doesn't give as much milk as Molly. I'll be glad when Molly has her calf and starts giving milk again."

Mr. Brinkman rinsed the bucket and put it out on the porch. "I'm just glad we have two cows. And if Molly's calf is a heifer we'll have enough cows to start selling our extra milk to neighbors in a couple of years." He sat down at the table.

Mrs. Brinkman began serving fried eggs and small moose steaks.

"What will we do with Molly's calf if he's a boy?" asked Blue-John.

"Sell him," answered his stepfather. "Or feed him for a year and then eat him."

"EAT him!" exclaimed Blue-John.

"Sure. Cut him up into steaks and hamburger. Yum yum!" Mr. Brinkman smiled wickedly and licked his lips.

"Well, for crying in a bucket!" exclaimed Blue-John.

Mrs. Brinkman sat down and they began breakfast.

"I'm sure glad I'm a girl," murmured Angie.

*   *   *

After breakfast Mr. Brinkman and Blue-John went to the potato patch to check the bear tracks.

"It's a grizzly, all right," said Mr. Brinkman, as he examined the bear tracks. "A brownie." He looked up and down the row of potatoes. He hefted his rifle. "Let's see where the tracks go," he said, and started down the row toward the woods. He and Blue-John followed the tracks into the forest of spruce and birch trees. The tracks were soon lost in the thick carpet of cranberry plants and moss that covered the ground under the trees. They left the woods and went back out into the potato patch.

Mr. Brinkman looked around. "Well, he's a pretty fair-sized bear. Probably a stray, passing through.

He might keep moving on. Or . . ."—Mr. Brinkman put his hands on his hips and squinted down the row of tracks—". . . judging from the size of these prints he's an old bear, maybe chased out of his old feeding territory by a younger, stronger bear. Too bad."

"Too bad? Why?" asked Blue-John.

"He'll be mean and cranky. His teeth could be worn down and abscessed. He'll wander cross-country until he finds territory that isn't claimed by some other bear."

"And he'll settle down there, huh?"

"Maybe. If he likes it. And until another bear comes along and chases him on again."

"Say!" exclaimed Blue-John. "There's no other bear here, on the homestead."

Mr. Brinkman was studying the forest. "Exactly. He might decide to move in here. Then I'd have to kill him."

"Kill him? But if he's an old guy couldn't we just let him stay around here? Maybe he wouldn't bother nobody. He didn't even look at me yesterday."

Mr. Brinkman shook his head. "Yesterday was the luckiest day of your life, John. That 'old guy' bear could have swatted you just once as he walked past and that would be all she wrote for John Charles Brinkman, sometimes called Blue-John, after he turned blue, while washing the dog one day." Mr. Brinkman grinned and started back to the house.

"Aw, Dad, ain't you never going to forget that? I ain't blue anymore." Blue-John had to hurry to keep up with his stepfather. "Well, maybe this old bear just ain't mean. Maybe he might like it so much here he just wouldn't bother nobody. Dad, you just gotta see him! He looks like the king of all bears!"

"If I see him, John, I'll have to shoot him, king or not. We can't have a grizzly on our farm."

"But why, Dad? Couldn't we just try it?"

"John, you don't 'just try' living with a grizzly bear," replied Mr. Brinkman sharply. "First he would be chasing us out of the fields, and then he would start killing our livestock, and then he would kill us. A king like him doesn't share things."

They were passing through the vegetable garden, and Mr. Brinkman bent to check the size of a cabbage plant.

"Now," he continued, "let's go make some hay. With the bear around I don't want you out here in the potato patch alone. You can help me for a few days, until we're sure the bear has left.

They went on to the house, but Blue-John stopped twice to look back at the woods where the bear had been.

Mr. Brinkman got a canteen of coffee to carry on

the tractor, and his rifle. He put the rifle in an old army scabbard and tied the scabbard to a fender on the tractor.

Blue-John watched him fill the tractor's fuel tank with gasoline.

Mr. Brinkman said, "I'll finish turning over the hay today. You get the hayloft ready. Pile up the old hay near the haydrop, and we'll feed it down first."

"Can I make a tunnel?" asked Blue-John.

"Yeah, sure," replied Mr. Brinkman. He put the gasoline can back in the tractor shed. "Then clean out the cow stalls. Better check the rabbit cages. They might need cleaning." He got up on the tractor. "And tomorrow we'll start bringing in the hay. I'm two weeks late with the hay anyway. Too much dog-gone rain."

He started the tractor. It snarled and popped and roared to life. "You and Angie stay close to the house." He waved good-by. "See you at lunch." The tractor roared as he drove out of the farm lot.

Blue-John went to the house. In the kitchen he sat down at the table to watch his mother empty the milk from the can into small buckets.

"What are you going to do today, brave son?" she asked.

"Oh, I dunno," replied Blue-John. "Nothing much."

"Well, you can help me. The chicken house needs

cleaning, and I wish you would look see if any berries are ripening early."

Blue-John got up. "Uh, I guess I better go get the hayloft ready for the new hay."

He went out to the barn. Molly was in her stall, and Mr. Brinkman had turned Ginger into the small meadow behind the barn and garden.

Blue-John leaned against Molly's stall. "Hi, cow," he said. "Say, I'll tell you something if you won't tell. You better have a girl calf. If you have a boy calf they're gonna eat him. What do you think of that?"

The cow was chewing a mouthful of hay, and looked calmly at the boy. "Well, don't say I didn't warn you," said Blue-John, going to the front of the barn. Just inside the front door was a ladder nailed to the wall. The ladder went up through a big square hole in the loft floor. The hole was the haydrop, where Blue-John pitched hay down each winter evening, and then pitched it into hayracks for Molly and Ginger. He went up the ladder.

The hayloft was Blue-John's favorite place on the homestead. He could hide from Angie in the hayloft. He could see over the tractor shed to the far side of the hayfield. In the late spring he watched swallows feeding their hungry young ones in a nest up in a corner of the roof. Standing in the big loft doorway in the end of the barn he felt much closer to the great white-headed eagles that soared in sweeping circles against the sky.

Through cracks in the floor he could look down on the cows in their stalls. From above, the cows looked like strange, prehistoric fish, with fat stomachs and no legs.

The loft was a good place to sit on a lazy summer day and eat a turnip, and listen to the mice squeaking in the oat bundles. Two years ago Blue-John's stepfather had grown oats as well as hay. A strange-looking machine had come and cut the oats. The machine had tied the oats in bundles and the bundles were loaded on a wagon and stacked in the barn loft. All of the bundles had been fed to the cows except for a row of them that were still leaning, like a fence, against the steep roof of the barn. There was a tunnel between the oat bundles and the roof, and when hay was piled in the barn, Blue-John could crawl down the tunnel and squirm up through the loose hay and come out at the end of the barn, on top of the hay.

A pulley was wired to the peak of the barn roof, above the loft door, and a long rope went through the pulley and hung to the ground. Sometimes, if Mr. Brinkman shot a moose when there was snow on the ground, he would drag the moose to the barn with the tractor and hoist it up with the rope, to skin it and butcher it. Most of the time one end of the rope was tied to the barn wall, and Blue-John used the other end to slide down out of the loft.

Blue-John got a fork and began pitching the old hay over toward the haydrop. He raked and pitched till he had most of the old hay piled around two sides of the haydrop. He stopped now and then to look for a raven that was calling from the forest. When he had the floor clear he stretched out on the floor and watched Molly in her stall below. He pushed stems of hay through the crack, aiming to drop them on Molly, and make her twitch one ear or the other.

Finally, he began straightening up the row of oat bundles. He moved two of the bundles.

On the floor, where a bundle had been, was a mouse nest. Most of the nest had stuck to the oat bundle when he moved it, but there were still wispy bits of hair, small feathers, and string and stuffing from an old insulated jacket that hung downstairs.

In the middle of the nest were three baby mice.

Blue-John got down on his hands and knees and cupped his chin in his hands to study them. They were pink, almost hairless, and smaller than lima beans. Their eyes were still tightly shut. They lay on their sides, helpless, hardly moving.

As Blue-John watched, he saw, out of the corner of his eye, a slight movement at the bottom of the next oat bundle.

He turned, and saw a mouse watching him.

As he watched, the mouse took a few quick steps toward the nest and then turned and darted back to the bundle. Again the mouse darted out, hesitated, and retreated. Blue-John realized it was the mother mouse, trying to rescue her babies.

Slowly he scooted backwards until he was more than an arm's length from the nest. The mother mouse watched him.

Then she darted out again, nervously watching the boy. She stopped midway to the nest, uncertain of the boy. He didn't move. She ran to the nest. Quickly she examined each tiny pink infant. Blue-John guessed she was smelling them. He was glad he had not touched them, which would have left his scent on them, and might have caused her to abandon them.

The mother mouse gently picked up one infant with her mouth and ran with it into the oat bundle. In a moment she appeared again, and like a quick, small shadow, darted to the nest and rescued the second infant. Again, a third time, she made a trip across the open floor to the nest, and picked up the last of her tiny babies, and took it to the safety of the oat bundle.

It was so quiet in the barn Blue-John could hear Molly munching hay downstairs.

Suddenly the silence was shattered by Burrs' barking outside. Startled, Blue-John jumped. He listened, and heard the tractor coming from the hayfield. He went to the loft door and saw his stepfather on the tractor halfway up the hayfield. Burrs was directly below, at the barn door, barking fiercely.

Blue-John looked down, and saw that Burrs wasn't barking a greeting to the tractor. Burrs was barking at something in the forest.

Blue-John looked toward the forest.

There, across the meadow, just outside the fence, watching Ginger, was the bear.

CHAPTER FOUR

Trapped

B LUE-JOHN reached for the rope to slide down
out of the hayloft. Burrs was barking hysterically.
The bear looked toward the barn. The bear began
moving, down along the rail fence, in the direction of
Ginger.

Blue-John slid down the rope and ran to the
meadow fence where it joined the barn. He vaulted
over the top rail as Burrs scooted under the bottom
rail, barking.

They started running across the meadow toward the
bear. Blue-John picked up a rock and ran on. He
was halfway across the meadow when he yelled, "Hey,
you, git!"

The bear stopped and looked at him. At the same
instant Ginger looked up and saw the bear. She threw
up her tail and ran, terrified, across the field.

Blue-John drew back his arm as if to throw the rock. Suddenly, the bear wheeled and disappeared into the forest. Burrs ran to the fence where the bear had been, barking and yapping as if he were telling the bear to come back and fight.

The boy went back to the barn, and soon Burrs followed him. Ginger was standing in a far corner of the meadow, eating grass.

Burrs ran into the yard, looking for the big white rooster. Blue-John went into the barn. He climbed to the loft and walked softly to the row of oat bundles. He picked up the bundle with the mouse nest on the bottom and very carefully put it back where it had been. Then he put back the other bundle.

He went to the loft door and waved to his stepfather, who was coming into the barnlot on the tractor. He slid down the rope and stood waiting.

"Hi, John," said Mr. Brinkman, as he got off the tractor. He bent and unbent his weak leg. "Got the loft all ready?"

"I guess so," replied his stepson. "I got the hay all moved."

They walked toward the house.

"Get the cow stalls cleaned?"

"Well, no."

"Or the rabbit cages?"

"Uh, well, no."

"Hmm," said Mr. Brinkman. "What did you do all morning?"

"Well, you know," answered Blue-John. "That hay-mow kept me pretty busy!"

"I'll just bet it did," said Mr. Brinkman, grinning. "What were you doing in the meadow, looking for mice?"

"Naw." Blue-John hesitated. "Uh—yeah."

His stepfather smiled and ruffled Blue-John's hair. "I'll bet you would put that grizzly bear in a cage in your room, if you could catch him. Let's eat lunch."

They went into the house.

* * *

After lunch Mr. Brinkman was in the tractor shed sharpening an ax. Blue-John walked in.

"What are you going to chop?" asked the boy.

"A spruce the wind blew down last week. Its top is laying over into the hayfield. Since the chain is broke on my chain saw I'll have to use this old toe-nail trimmer." He rasped a heavy file across the edge of the ax.

"Dad, I been thinking, and there's something I ought to tell you. About this morning . . ."

"Tell me later, can you, John? Right now I wish you'd get the canteen off the tractor and have your mother fill it with coffee."

Blue-John started out to the tractor. His stepfather

called, "No, wait, John. How would you like to go out with me and we'll start picking up hay this afternoon?"

"Hot dog!" shouted the boy.

"The hay is cured out enough on the south side of the field."

Blue-John ran to get the canteen.

"Have your mother put water in the canteen, then," called Mr. Brinkman. He examined the edge of the ax. He laid down the heavy file and carried the ax to the tractor. He slid the rifle out of its scabbard and slipped the ax into the scabbard, handle first. He went into the tractor shed and reaching up, laid the rifle on a board high up on the side of the wall. Then he put some cans of paint and old nails on the shelf, to hide the rifle from the children.

Later that afternoon, bleeding and helpless, he would face the great brown bear with only a hammer in his hand, with the rifle on its shelf, hidden behind the cans of paint and nails.

He started to pick up the can of gasoline to fill the tractor's fuel tank.

Blue-John called, "How about taking a couple of turnips out with us to eat?"

"Good idea," Mr. Brinkman called back. "Did you remember to give Molly some water this morning?"

"Gee, I forgot."

"I'll do it," called Mr. Brinkman, and he put down the gasoline can. He went to the well and pumped a bucket of water and took it into the barn. When he came out Blue-John was waiting at the tractor.

"Can I back it up to the wagon?" asked the boy.

"Better not," answered his stepfather as he climbed up on the tractor. "The clutch in this old clunk is getting bad. It's easy to kill the engine. You put the pin in. Okay?"

He started the tractor and eased it back to the wagon. Blue-John pulled a long bolt from a hole in the hitch on the tractor. His stepfather eased the tractor back until the hole in the tractor hitch lined up with a hole in the wagon tongue. Then the boy dropped the bolt through the holes, hooking the wagon to the tractor.

Blue-John climbed up on the tractor and leaned against a fender. They drove out of the barn lot.

The tractor and wagon sailed down the hayfield, straddling a windrow of hay. Blue-John enjoyed the cool wind stinging his face, and watched the trees in the forest slipping past. The tractor was like a great monster bull, charging down the field, eating up an endless row of hay.

Blue-John put his hand on the rifle scabbard. "Dad," he yelled above the noise of the tractor. "You didn't bring the gun!"

"No," Mr. Brinkman yelled back. "Won't need it. That bear's probably miles away by now."

"But, Dad . . ." Blue-John started to say.

"Anyway," his stepfather grinned, slapping the gun case—"makes a handy place to carry an ax.

They rode on in silence. Again Blue-John watched the forest slipping past, but now he was anxiously looking for something, hoping not to see it.

Mr. Brinkman nudged Blue-John and pointed to two cow moose eating hay near the woods. He turned the wheel and aimed the tractor toward the moose. They looked up and studied the approaching tractor, then went on eating.

Mr. Brinkman roared up to the moose and gunned the engine. The animals wheeled and began trotting down the row of hay. Mr. Brinkman chased them with the tractor.

"Eeeyah! Yah! Yah! Git along there, moose!" yelled Blue-John and his stepfather. Yelling and shouting, they chased the moose until the animals suddenly veered into the forest.

Mr. Brinkman drove to the end of the field and turned to pull up beside a windrow of hay.

"Doggone big-nose hayrustlers will have the hay eaten up before we can get it to the barn," laughed Mr. Brinkman. "And then they'll come around wanting handouts this winter." He got out of the tractor seat. "Okay, moose wrangler, it's your turn to pilot this thing."

Blue-John slipped into the seat and put the tractor in gear.

"Leave it in low gear and let the clutch out easy. If you let it out too fast you'll kill the engine." He got down and took a pitchfork from the hayrack on the front of the wagon.

He pitched hay onto the wagon until he had loaded all the hay that was near the wagon. Blue-John pulled the wagon ahead and his stepfather again loaded the hay.

They had gone partway down the field when Mr. Brinkman suddenly stuck his fork in the ground and yelled, "Gasoline! It's been gnawing at me that I forgot something. Now I remember! I didn't fill the gas tank back at the shed." He put his hands on his hips and shook his head. "Well, there's enough to get us one load of hay to the barn. Then we'll gas up." He began pitching hay again.

Slowly they worked across the end of the field. At the end of the row they stopped.

"Shut it off, John, and let's take a break. Bring the canteen and turnips."

Blue-John shut off the tractor and got down. They sat with their backs against the tractor wheel and each took a drink from the canteen. They munched turnips.

The sun was warm but the air was cool. A ceiling of thin, gray clouds was slowly inching across the pale blue sky. To the east the Kenai Mountains loomed up dark and jagged.

A raven landed on a fence post. It looked at the tractor, and wagon, and man, and boy, and lazily flew away.

"What are you going to name your calf, John?" asked Mr. Brinkman.

"I don't know," answered the boy. "Can't think of anything I like."

"Well, it's due in two or three days, you know."

"Oh, I might name it for the day it's born. You know, like Tuesday, or Sunday, or something." Blue-John took another drink of water.

"Well, that's something different, all right. Never heard of a cow named Saturday." Mr. Brinkman chuckled. He looked down at the boy. " 'Course, I never heard of a boy being named Blue-John, either." He threw a pebble at his boot. "How did you ever get such a name? I forgot."

"Aw, Dad, you ain't forgot. I don't guess you'll ever forget."

"That was about the funniest thing I ever saw,

John. You trying to give Burrs a bath that day, and him not wanting it. You and Burrs and a whole box of laundry soap in Molly's watering trough. So many suds we couldn't see either of you—and the water was blue from the color that bleached out of your brand-new denims and you were blue from head to toe, hair and all—and blue for days!"

"For crying in a bucket, Dad! That was two years ago!" Blue-John looked away. "Geeee whiz!" He turned back grinning. "Well, I sure got old Burrs clean, didn't I?"

"Sure did!" laughed his stepfather, bouncing another pebble off his boot. " 'Course, Burrs was blue for a while, too."

It was the last time he would wear that boot, for within an hour the ax in the rifle scabbard would bite, quick and hard, into the worn brown leather.

"Dad—uh, I just gotta tell you about this morning."

"Oh, took a nap, huh? Well, that hayloft makes a guy sleepy."

Blue-John retied one of his tennis shoes. "No. I mean about being out in the meadow. I was—chasing the bear."

"What!" Mr. Brinkman sat straight up and stared at his stepson.

"Aw, I really didn't chase it. I just ran out and yelled and it went away."

"What was it doing?"

"Well," said Blue-John, "sort of looking—at Ginger, I think."

"At *Ginger*!"

"Uh, yeah." Blue-John shifted uncomfortably. "Through the fence."

Mr. Brinkman frowned. "I don't like the looks of it. First he walks right past you in the spud patch. Then he comes up to the fence and looks Ginger over."

He stood up. "Looks like he might be thinking of moving in on us. Let's not be sitting out here in the hayfield."

He climbed up on the tractor, started it, and turned the corner of the field. He left the tractor idling, climbed down, and took the pitchfork Blue-John had brought along.

"When you get to the fallen tree just pull out around it and I'll chop off the top of it." He started pitching hay onto the wagon.

A short distance ahead of the tractor was the spruce that had been blown down. Its top lay across the first windrow of hay.

Sitting on the tractor, Blue-John was worried and silent. He knew he should have told his stepfather about the bear at lunchtime. Maybe the bear hadn't decided to move on. Maybe it was thinking of staying on the homestead. He swept his eyes around the borders of the homestead, looking for the bear. He thought of the great, old, shaggy monarch, slowly stalking through the woods around the farm, homeless, hungry.

"Hey, John! Daydreaming?" called his stepfather. "Move it on."

Blue-John drove the tractor ahead. His stepfather continued pitching hay onto the wagon.

Blue-John wondered about the bear. Was it mean enough to attack people, as his stepfather had said? If the bear couldn't find food would he come out of the woods some day, and catch someone in a field, or his mother in the yard feeding the chickens, or Angie in the barn?

He looked back. His stepfather waved him on again. He moved ahead.

Blue-John rested his hand on the ax head sticking out of the gun case. It was cold. He wished his stepfather had brought the rifle.

"Say, Dad, where *is* the rifle, anyway?"

Mr. Brinkman paused. Perhaps, he thought, it would be wise to tell Blue-John where the rifle was, since the bear was prowling around the farm. "In the tractor shed, up on a shelf, behind some paint cans," he replied.

"Is it loaded?" asked the boy.

"Sure is, so don't touch it unless you really need it, understand?"

"Don't worry!"

"And don't tell Angie." Mr. Brinkman went back to pitching hay.

"I won't!"

Soon Mr. Brinkman motioned Blue-John to move ahead. They had reached the fallen tree and Blue-John angled the tractor around the top of the tree. Mr. Brinkman cleared away the hay around the tree and threw it on the wagon.

"Okay, John, pull ahead some more and shut off the tractor. And bring back the ax." Mr. Brinkman began throwing loose branches out of the way.

Blue-John brought the ax. Its sharp edge gleamed in the sunlight.

Mr. Brinkman studied the tree. "Guess we can cut this top into two pieces and drag them out of the way." He stepped up to the long, slender tree and began chopping a wedge-shaped cut into the trunk. He swung the ax in smooth, shining arcs. It bit into the tree each time with a hard, quick smack, and chips of wood flew.

He finished the first cut through the trunk, and stepped back, leaning on the ax handle.

"Okay, John. See if you can drag that much over to the edge of the field."

He limped down to the next place to make a cut. "This busted-up leg ain't much for swinging an ax," he said, stopping to rub his leg.

He began chopping.

Blue-John started to drag away the piece of tree top, around the other side of the tree. He had dragged it almost to the edge of the field.

Suddenly Mr. Brinkman gave a quick, hoarse gasp.

Blue-John looked up.

His stepfather was bent over, gripping the ax. His face was pale, and had a strange look Blue-John had never seen before. He seemed to be tugging at the ax. The ax seemed to be stuck in something.

Blue-John stared, trying to see through the tree branches.

Abruptly his stepfather jerked the ax loose, and threw it aside.

The blade was bright red.

Mr. Brinkman staggered back and fell.

Blue-John rushed around the tree. His stepfather was breathing in great, hoarse gasps. Mr. Brinkman jerked to a sitting position and grabbed his right boot. Blood was spurting from a long gash in the toe of the boot. He squeezed the boot together and blood ran out on his hands. His teeth were clenched. He was moaning softly.

Blue-John knelt beside him. "Oh—Dad!"

Mr. Brinkman gripped his leg below the knee and lifted it. "Get—get the boot off!"

Blue-John took hold of the bloody boot and pulled gently.

"Pull!" commanded his stepfather. "Don't worry—about—hurting me."

Blue-John gripped the boot with both hands and yanked. His hands slipped on the blood-soaked leather and he fell back.

"Pull!"

He grabbed the boot again and pulled. His step-father drew in a long gasp of air through his clenched teeth.

The boot slipped off. Mr. Brinkman grabbed his foot with both hands and squeezed it together.

"Got to bind it with something," he said. "Got a handkerchief?"

Blue-John shook his head. Then he jumped up and ripped off his shirt. He skinned off his tee shirt and knelt down. With trembling fingers he tried to make a bandage. The blood made everything slippery. He couldn't seem to make his fingers and thumbs work right. Finally he managed to get the tee shirt bound tightly around his stepfather's bleeding foot.

"I put too much weight on my bad leg and it folded up on me," said Mr. Brinkman. "Slipped. Couldn't get—my foot out of the way—of the ax."

He looked around. "Help me over to the tractor."

He leaned on his stepson and they hobbled to the tractor. Mr. Brinkman was heavy and Blue-John almost fell under his weight several times. When they reached the tractor Mr. Brinkman sat on the hitch bar.

"Drive it, John. I'll ride the hitch." He eased the bleeding foot onto the hitch. "Pull the pin and leave the wagon here. Get it later."

Blue-John pulled the long bolt out of the tractor hitch and pushed the wagon tongue out of the way. He boarded the tractor and started the engine. He was very nervous. His hands felt sweaty, and his foot trembled on the clutch pedal. He looked around to check on his stepfather.

"Ready, Dad?"

"Let her rip, John." He was holding to the base of the tractor seat with one hand and trying to squeeze the bleeding foot with the other. Blood was dripping slowly onto the hitch.

Blue-John put the tractor in gear and let out the clutch.

The tractor lurched. The engine died.

Nervously the boy shoved the gear lever into neutral. He pushed in the clutch and reached for the starter.

"That's all right, John," Mr. Brinkman said gently. "Just relax a little. Give it more gas when you let out the clutch." His voice was quiet and confident. "Just give it more gas. I'll hang on."

Blue-John yanked down on the gas feed, a small lever in front of the steering wheel. He pulled out the choke knob, and pushed the starter.

The starter whined but the engine wouldn't start.

Blue-John frantically jerked the gas lever up and down and pressed the starter.

"Better let up for a minute, John," called his stepfather. "You'll flood the engine." His voice sounded a little tense now, and strained.

Blue-John turned off the key and let out the clutch. His leg trembled and his foot slipped off the clutch with a thump. His hands were damp with sweat, and small beads of sweat lined his upper lip. He looked around at his stepfather. Mr. Brinkman was squeezing his foot with both hands.

Slowly his stepfather said, "We'll let the gas drain out of the carburetor and try it again, in a minute." He smiled at Blue-John, and winked.

Blue-John nodded. He couldn't speak. He wanted to say something, to apologize for his clumsiness, to tell his stepfather how sorry he was that he was hurt, to do something, anything, that would magically solve everything. But he could think of nothing. He felt like a lump of wood, useless, sitting on the tractor seat.

He slumped down defeated, trembling, fighting back tears.

Suddenly he leaped from the tractor and began running toward home.

"The truck!" he shouted back. "I'll get Mom to bring the pickup." His voice faded as he raced across the field. "Be right back, Dad!"

Mr. Brinkman leaned back against the tractor. His foot throbbed and pain flashed through his leg like an electric current, but the bleeding had slowed down. He closed his eyes. He knew Blue-John would run all the way to the house, and would be back soon.

For a moment he tried to relax. There was not a sound in the hayfield, not even a raven calling. There was not a breath of wind.

Suddenly he opened his eyes. He had a feeling something was wrong, a sense of danger approaching. He sat up and looked around. He could not see around the tractor wheel, so he stood up on his one good leg and peered around the wheel.

Coming across the hayfield, toward the tractor, was the bear.

CHAPTER FIVE

Rescue

THE bear stopped, halfway to the tractor. A massive mountain of brown fur, he stood perfectly still, studying Mr. Brinkman. The sunlight gleamed like ancient, yellow dust on his small ears and shoulder hump. His small, bright, black eyes watched the man intently.

Mr. Brinkman gripped the ax. Since he couldn't stand squarely to swing the ax he knew it was useless, but he would go down fighting. He thought of the rifle lying on the shelf in the toolshed. He realized with a shock that his wife and Angie and Blue-John didn't know about the bear. They would have no weapon when they came to help him. The bear might attack them, too, he feared.

The blood dripping from his foot was forming a glistening red pool on the ground. The tractor hitch was spattered with blood. Mr. Brinkman guessed the bear could smell the blood, or see it. Could the bear sense he was badly injured, maybe helpless? All the bear had to do was walk in and get him.

The bear took a few steps forward. The sun glinted dully on his long heavy claws.

Mr. Brinkman got a small wrench from the toolbox above his head. He grabbed the tractor seat and pulled himself up. He thought maybe there was one chance in a thousand that the bear could be scared away. He suddenly felt dizzy. He swayed unsteadily. He gripped the tractor seat to steady himself, and threw the wrench. It sailed, spinning and shining, in an arc, and bounced along the ground in front of the bear. At the same time Mr. Brinkman yelled, "Git! Git out of here!" and waved an arm.

The bear paid no attention. He came on, walking slowly, but directly toward the tractor.

Mr. Brinkman looked for a way to pull himself up on the tractor. He laid the ax up on the floor of the tractor. Then, gripping the tractor seat, he started to pull himself up. He hopped, and got his left foot up on the hitch, but the hitch was slippery with blood, and his foot slipped off.

He fell back against the tractor wheel, and accidentally hit the ax. The ax slid off the floor and thumped to the ground near the tractor's front wheels.

It lay beyond his reach.

Mr. Brinkman leaned against the wheel, weak and suddenly sick. His foot throbbed. The pain knifed through him. He fumbled in the toolbox, and drew out a heavy ballpeen hammer.

He gripped the hammer, and turned to face the bear.

The bear had stopped, and was looking toward the house.

Mr. Brinkman turned, but he couldn't see the house. The tractor was in the way. But he knew what the bear was watching, for now he could hear the pick-up coming.

Holding to the tractor wheel for support, he hobbled around to the side of the tractor, where he could see.

The truck was roaring down the field, bouncing and swaying. Angie was in front with Mrs. Brinkman, and Blue-John was in the back. The truck bounced to a stop next to the tractor and Mrs. Brinkman and Blue-John leaped out.

"Just help me in the truck and let's get out of here," shouted Mr. Brinkman. "The bear . . . the bear . . . !"

"I saw the bear. That bear can just go look somewhere else," said Mrs. Brinkman, firmly. "You're losing too much blood." She had brought a bed sheet and she tore off a long, wide strip. She bent down and took his injured foot in her lap. She took off the blood-soaked bandage and tossed it into the back of the pickup. Then she quickly began binding the foot with the strip of sheet.

"In the truck! We don't know what that bear is going to do—wrap it up in the truck!" insisted Mr. Brinkman.

Mrs. Brinkman hesitated. "But, who will drive?"

"John can! Even if he has to go all the way in low gear!"

Mrs. Brinkman got up. "All right. Lean on me." She helped him up and they started to the truck. "John! John, quick!" she called. "Oh, where did that boy *go?*"

Blue-John came running around the front of the tractor.

"Where is the bear? Coming or going?" asked Mr. Brinkman.

"Going," answered Blue-John. "Toward the woods."

"Smart bear," said Mrs. Brinkman, helping her husband into the back of the pickup. "He knew better than to tangle with us Brinkmans."

"That's probably the real truth. Too many people, and the truck. Scared him away," said Mr. Brinkman. "Well, come on, let's get out of here."

Mrs. Brinkman got into the back of the truck. "I think I'd better wash out the cut before I bind it,

Honey. So John had better drive, anyway. John, bring the canteen of water from the tractor, and then you drive."

Blue-John brought the canteen of water to his mother, then got into the pickup. Angie stared at him, wide-eyed.

He put the truck in gear and gripped the steering wheel. He had to stretch to see over the hood, and his foot trembled on the clutch.

Then his stepfather called, "Sure glad you can drive it, John. We'd be in a bind, without you. Give it heck!"

Remembering the tractor, Blue-John slowly let out the clutch and mashed the gas pedal to the floor. With a roar, the truck leaped forward. It bucked and lurched as he made a circle around the tractor and wagon and went roaring down the field in low gear, until, with the engine screaming and the gears clashing, Blue-John got the shift lever into second gear, and then into third.

The bear stood in the field, watching them, and then slowly padded into the forest.

The truck roared into the barn lot. When Blue-John reached the house he abruptly jammed on the brakes. Everyone in the truck lurched forward.

Angie looked at Blue-John scornfully. "Some driver!" she said.

He grinned weakly. "Well, I got here. What do you want, anyway? My gosh!" He shut off the engine and got out.

Mrs. Brinkman was finishing the bandage on her husband's foot. She tore thin strips off the sheet and tied the bandage securely. "How does it feel?" she asked.

"Like my foot's about to fall off," replied Mr. Brinkman. He squirmed uncomfortably. "How about putting something soft under this foot. John, run fill a gunny sack with hay."

Blue-John ran to the barn.

Mr. Brinkman continued. "We'll stop at Tex Doan's, and tell him what's happened. Since there is no doctor in these parts we'll have to drive to Kenai and radio for the Air Rescue plane to come from Anchorage for me. You might be late getting home. I'd like for Tex to keep an eye on things with the bear around. He could milk Ginger, too."

He rubbed his hand over his face. "Your brother Kirk can come out and help you with the haying. Blue-John can do the chores, milk Ginger, and clean out the cow stalls." He slapped the side of the truck. "How could I be so careless with that ax?"

Mrs. Brinkman put her hand on his arm. "Don't fret about it, Honey. It just happened. It could be a lot worse. The kids and I will be all right. John and

I can start the generator. And Kirk isn't salmon fishing right now. He has a couple of days between catches. He's just working on his boat and patching nets. He can come out and stay, if I need help."

Mr. Brinkman grumbled. "Well, it was a black day on the Alaska Highway when that bulldozer rolled over and wrinkled up my leg."

Blue-John came running back with the sack of hay. He gave it to his mother. As Mrs. Brinkman tenderly lifted her husband's foot and rested it on the sack she looked at Mr. Brinkman and said softly, "Honey, if the army hadn't sent you up here to help build that road, that dozer wouldn't have smashed your leg, and you wouldn't have been sent to the hospital in Anchorage, and you wouldn't have met the widow Christine Benteen and her son, John Charles, and married her, and had a daughter name of Angie, and you wouldn't have settled on this homestead, and just *think*, you wouldn't be on that homestead, sitting in a truck, in August, 1952, with your foot split open and ready to fall *off*!"

She took a deep breath, laughing, and hugged him, and gave him a noisy kiss.

Mr. Brinkman was cheered up, and smacked her on the seat of the pants. "You're a nut," he laughed. "Blue-John," he commanded, "drive this fancy limousine over to Tex Doan's. Your mother and I aim to look over our—estate." He winked at Blue-John. Mrs. Brinkman sat down beside him.

Blue-John grinned and got into the truck.

Angie gasped. "Oh, no, you're not going to drive again?"

"Sure," answered the boy nonchalantly. He started the engine, put the truck in gear, and with a leap and a roar, went bouncing out of the driveway and down the long narrow lane toward the highway.

They passed the hayfield where the tractor and wagon had been abandoned. Next they passed a flat, spongy bog, where two moose stood, watching them. The lane was rough, rutted, and narrow. It had been gouged out of the bush country by the three homestead families who had been moved into the area. The Brinkmans lived at the end of the lane. Next was Augie "Tex" Doan's place. Nearest the highway was an abandoned homestead, once owned by the Rafferty family. The Raffertys had given up years ago and had gone back to Michigan. Now alders and willows choked the barn lot, and spruces and birches were beginning to sprout in the oatfield.

In a moment Blue-John turned in to Tex Doan's homestead. Again, when he reached the house he abruptly jammed on the brakes and again everyone in the truck lurched forward.

Angie didn't even look at her stepbrother this time.

She just stared in disgust out the window and said, "Well, you did it again."

"Aw, for crying in a bucket!" muttered Blue-John as they both got out of the truck.

A large, stout woman stepped out of the house. She was wearing blue denims, a plaid shirt, and cowboy boots. Her face was tanned and her black hair was streaked with gray.

Mrs. Brinkman stood up to meet her. "Hi, Belle," she said.

"Well, look at y'all," cried Mrs. Doan, striding up to the truck. "Riding around in the back end of a pickup like two hogs going to market." She peered into the back of the truck and stopped short when she saw Mr. Brinkman's foot.

"Oh my, oh my!" she gasped. "Will, Honey, what on *earth* did y'all do to your foot?"

"Chewed my toenail too much," answered Mr. Brinkman with a weak grin.

"He split it with an ax, Belle, chopping wood," sighed Mrs. Brinkman, getting out of the truck. "We're on our way to Kenai to call for an Air Rescue plane from Anchorage. We wondered if Tex could keep an eye on our place this evening. I might get back late."

"Why, surely, Chris. Tex would be glad to," replied Mrs. Doan. She whirled and called toward a large shedlike building. "Hey, Tex! Git out from under that cat and git over here!" She turned back to the Brinkmans. "He's putting a new hydraulic jimcrack or something on the bulldozer."

She whirled around again, drew in a deep breath and yelled so loud that Blue-John and Angie ducked. "Hey, you bow-legged cat-skinner! August Ambrose DOAN! Git OVER here! We got a 'mergency! This hickory-head Will Brinkman chopped his hoof in half with a ax! You hear? Will Brinkman!"

She turned to Mr. Brinkman and smiled apologetically. "When he's under that dozer with his ears full of grease he just don't hear good. I'll go fetch him."

She started for the shed and stopped when a figure appeared, coming out. He wiped his hands on a big rag and came trotting toward the truck. He was short, and tanned, and his bald head glistened with sweat, except where it was smudged with grease. He wore denim pants and shirt, and greasy cowboy boots.

"Well, it's about time," scowled Mrs. Doan.

Tex Doan ignored her. He trotted up to the pickup and looked in. "Who done what?" he asked. He saw Will Brinkman's foot, and whistled. "How did you go to do that? If the size of the wrapping on your foot means anything you'll never *walk* again!"

"Oh, it's not cut that bad," grinned Mr. Brinkman.

"Christine just happened to have a whole bed sheet so she just wrapped most of it on the foot." He shifted his foot on the sack of hay. "Hey, Tex, do me a favor? It will take a while to get an Air Rescue plane from Anchorage, and Christine will get home late. Could you go over about dark and chase Ginger into the barn and milk her and throw her down some hay? Better lock the barn. Got an old brownie prowling around and he's getting nosey. Close the chicken coop, too, will you?"

Tex Doan half turned and spat a long brown jet of tobacco juice. "Y'all going to Kenai to get a plane? What in thunder for? That'll take hours! Seward's got a hospital and I can get you there in an hour flat. In *my* plane!" He clapped Will Brinkman on the shoulder. "Boy, y'all cut me to the quick. Just going to drive right on past poor old Tex, and him with a airplane just a-sitting here, wanting to fly."

He ran a calloused, greasy hand over his bald head. "And it ain't ever' day I git a chance to break away from that foghorn I married."

He ducked as his wife swung at him. "Why, you runty little horny toad, I'll knock you clear into next Tuesday," she howled. "This boy is nigh to bleeding to death and you stand there jawing." She let down the truck's tail-gate and got in. "Don't just *stand* there, hammerhead! Let's fetch him to the plane. Tromp on it, Christine! Just drive right up to the plane."

Mr. Brinkman looked helplessly at his wife. "Looks like we've got no choice."

Tex Doan, Blue-John, and Angie scrambled into the back of the truck. Mrs. Brinkman got in front and drove around the bulldozer shed. There was a small yellow plane parked near the end of a long, smooth hayfield. The hay had been cut and the field was covered with a short, brown stubble.

Tex and his wife helped Mr. Brinkman out of the truck and over to the plane. It was a high-wing plane, with two seats in front and a small seat in back. They eased Mr. Brinkman into one of the front seats.

"Now, young fella, y'all just make yourself comfortable while I look around this here airplane to make sure all the pieces is here," said Tex Doan.

He started inspecting the outside of the plane while the Brinkmans and Mrs. Doan talked. "Hey, there, High-pockets," he called to Blue-John. "Come on. Help me look for any missing parts, like the tail, or something." Shyly, Blue-John followed him around the plane as the man inspected the wings, and body, and looked at the tires, and propeller, and jiggled and thumped the plane here and there.

"The thing is, Johnboy," he said, spitting tobacco juice, "ever so often pieces just up and fall off these here airplanes. Why, I mind the time I was flying and the dern wings just up and fell off. Both of them. Just like that!" He spat again.

Blue-John stared at him, openmouthed.

"Sure did make it hard to fly, too. Had to hold out my arms for wings." He squinted down the wing and said quietly, " 'Course, the hard part was steering with my feet. Wasn't time to take off my boots."

He checked the engine oil and the engine, closed the cowling around the engine, and walked back to the cabin of the plane and threw open the door.

"Well, co-pilot," he said to Blue-John, "y'all git in and we'll go." Blue-John stared at him. Mr. and Mrs. Brinkman grinned, thinking Tex was kidding.

"Here, hop in back," repeated Tex. "Little seat back there just made for small britches."

Blue-John peered timidly into the plane.

Mr. Brinkman said, "You serious, Tex? About taking John?"

"Never been more serious. Y'all know I never kid."

"Oh, but Tex, he's never been up before," interrupted Mrs. Brinkman.

"Then it's high time he started," said Tex, spitting. He saw Mrs. Brinkman was worried. "Now, don't y'all fret, Christine. I been flying this here peninsula for

75

years and ain't lost a boy yet. It's a clear, cool day, perfect for flying. And I could fly over to Seward and back blindfolded."

"Oh, Tex, I'm not worried about your flying. You could fly a barn door in a blizzard. It's just . . ." She hesitated, and looked at her husband.

Mr. Brinkman shrugged. "It's okay with me," he grinned.

Tex Doan let out a whoop. "All settled, then. I'll just git my parachute." He reached into the plane and pulled out a battered cowboy hat and put it on. "There. Ten gallon parachute." He winked at Blue-John. He smacked the boy on the seat of the pants and helped him into the plane. "Just cinch up that belt around you good and tight, and grab a hold."

He got in. "Only thing I ask is, don't grab me around the neck when we land. Hear?"

Blue-John fastened the seat-belt around his waist. His mother leaned in and kissed him. She patted him on the knee. "Well, young eagle, this has turned out to be quite a day, hasn't it?" She smiled.

Blue-John smiled and nodded.

Tex Doan was checking the controls of the plane, and the fuel.

Mrs. Brinkman kissed her husband. "We'll come over and visit you, soon as we can. Tex can find out how bad your foot is, and how long you'll be in the hospital. Don't worry, Honey, we'll take care of things around here."

"I'm not worried," replied Mr. Brinkman. "In fact, I just might stay in Seward for the silver salmon derby. So long, Hon." He lifted Angie and kissed her. "Take care of your mother."

"Well, if y'all are through with your jawing and kissing good-by we can leave anytime," interrupted Tex Doan. "Hey, Belle, ain't you going to kiss me?"

"Kiss *you*, you homely coyote?" called Mrs. Doan. "Go on, git out of here!"

Mrs. Brinkman took Angie in her arms and the women stepped back.

"Be back by supper time," called Tex Doan, and he started the engine. He checked the gauges on the instrument panel, and let the engine warm up. He taxied the plane forward and checked the brakes, and revved up the engine.

Blue-John peeked out the window. The spinning propeller blew wind through the open doors into his face. His mother and Angie were waving. Angie was calling something but he couldn't hear her.

Then Tex Doan closed his door and Mr. Brinkman closed his. Tex taxied the plane to the end of the flight strip and pointed the plane down the runway.

Blue-John craned his neck to look back. His mother, and Angie, and Mrs. Doan were watching. For an instant, Blue-John wished he was standing there with them, and not going at all.

"Well, boys," called Tex Doan above the noise of the engine. "Let's us sashay on over to Seward, huh?" He revved up the engine and the little plane began rolling bumpily down the hayfield. Blue-John sat motionless in the tiny back seat, watching the brown hay stubble flashing past underneath.

His stomach felt strangely empty and hollow. He swallowed a dry swallow and held tightly to the seat.

Suddenly the plane stopped bumping. It seemed to be floating, smoothly and lightly. The hay stubble seemed to be falling away from the plane.

With a roar the plane lifted into the air.

CHAPTER SIX

Magic Yellow Wings

THE small yellow plane had broken its bond with the earth and was climbing, roaring with power as Tex Doan opened the throttle.

Blue-John watched the earth falling away from them. They were above the trees now, reaching for the sky. They crossed a bog. Blue-John recognized two moose as they started to run from the sound of the plane. They seemed to be running in slow motion, limber-legged and graceful, and looked like they were skimming lightly over the top of the peat moss in the bog. He felt that he could reach down and touch them, and pick them up.

They passed over a hayfield, where someone had left a tractor, and a wagon half full of brown hay. They were over a homestead now, still climbing and beginning to turn. A wingtip swung down as the plane banked around the homestead.

Blue-John gripped the seat more tightly and clenched his teeth. The plane felt as if it were going to tip over and go sliding down to the ground. He tried to balance himself by leaning toward the outside.

"Feel like you're about to tip over and fall off the fence, High-pockets?" called Tex Doan. "Don't fret. It always feels like that, first few times." He laughed. Mr. Brinkman turned around and smiled reassuringly.

Blue-John felt better. He continued to lean, hoping Tex Doan wouldn't notice. He loosened up, and studied the homestead below. There was a house, and a shed, and a log barn. Some tiny white things were scurrying around in the yard next to the house. Chickens! He realized with a shock that it was *his* house! He looked for Ginger and found her, in a far corner of the pasture. He thought of Molly in the barn, soon to have her calf.

The homestead looked like a set of toys, with the little house and log barn, and tiny animals. He spotted the open door of the hayloft, and the rope, hanging like a string from the barn peak. He remembered standing in that hayloft door, jealous of the eagles, watching them sweep and circle in the clear blue sky.

Now, suddenly, this day, here and now, he was up where the eagles flew, circling and sweeping in the same blue sky, looking down on the homestead, and the fields, and the bogs, and the woods.

The plane had circled the homestead and was sweeping southward, still climbing. As the plane straightened out Blue-John relaxed, and traced the lane to Tex Doan's place. He saw the truck, and the Doans' truck. Then he saw his mother, and Angie, and Mrs. Doan walking from the flight strip to the Doan house. He thought it was strange that he didn't feel like a boy in an airplane. Instead, he felt like a giant with magic wings, and he could reach down and touch the toys spread out below. Strange. And wonderful.

Tex Doan pointed the small yellow plane toward the jagged blue wall of the Kenai Mountains. Far to the left, below, was the small town of Sterling, with the little one-room log school Blue-John attended. They crossed the main highway to Anchorage and headed across the trackless bush country. The rolling hills were shaggy with the dark green of spruce trees, and splashed with the bright, pale green of aspen and birch. Blue lakes shimmered in the sun, and scattered between the hills were flat, treeless bogs, like brownish-green patches of soft fur.

Tex Doan opened the top half of his door and spat tobacco juice. Cold wind surged in and pierced Blue-John's denim shirt. Tex closed the door. "Guess I've splattered tobacco juice on half the peninsula from this here airplane," he said. "That's what makes all

81

them bare patches down there. The juice kills ever'
tree it hits. If I fly long enough I'll make a prairie
out of this here peninsula."

Blue-John grinned. He recalled the time his father
had dug down into a bog, to see how deep it was.
Mr. Brinkman had gouged out a hole six feet deep.
There had been no soil at all. Just solid peat moss.
It might have been peat moss twenty feet deep. Mr.
Brinkman quit digging and filled the hole. Blue-John
thought the bog didn't smell like tobacco juice.

They roared on. Tex Doan and Mr. Brinkman talked
about hunting, and watched for landmarks. Blue-John
watched the vast range of earth unfold below. They
were alone in the immense, clear, blue sky. Like a
fleeting, snarling intruder in the domain of hunting
eagles and horizon-bound geese, the yellow plane
raced toward the mountains.

Blue-John watched the plane's shadow racing with
it, over the trees, across the bogs, skipping lightly
across small streams and the river, but always firmly
bound to the earth. Blue-John found himself feeling
sorry for the shadow, bound to the earth.

He wondered if the mighty grizzlies, wandering
gruff and solitary in their ancient hunting lands, felt
the shadow as it touched them.

They approached the long, blue curve of a large
lake, deep and wind-wrinkled. "Skilak Lake," an-

nounced Tex Doan. "Too bad we ain't got time to stop and fish."

They sailed across the curve of the lake and headed for an opening between two massive mountains.

"Resurrection Pass dead ahead," called out Tex Doan. "I feel like a dadburn bus driver, calling out bus-stops." He opened his upper door half and spat. "Thing is, I don't want High-pockets to know I'm really *lost*!" He and Mr. Brinkman laughed, and they went on talking.

The plane swept lightly through the pass and soon approached another, smaller lake. They passed over the lake and headed down a wide, curving canyon. A river snaked through the bottom of the canyon, like a ribbon of wax. Mountains stood all about them now, treeless and wind-swept, above timberline. Small patches of snow lay in the deeper pockets of rock, feeding thin white streams of water that fell, lacy and silvery, down the rough brown flanks of the mountains.

Trim white sheep and bearded goats watched them from narrow ledges and outcroppings high on the mountain walls.

They passed a soaring eagle and Tex Doan yelled to it, "Hey! Want to race?"

They raced on, magic yellow wings carrying them over the top of the world, it seemed to Blue-John. Great, hulking, forbidding mountains rushed to challenge their magic, and were conquered and left behind.

Blue-white creeks tumbled down out of small, hidden canyons and met the river and joined it, and the waxen river grew a little each time.

Then trees and bushes began appearing on the mountains. Blue-John guessed they were getting close to the town of Seward, and he began watching for the ocean.

Suddenly he saw it, a flat, level, blue sea, just over the last rim of green mountains. The sky was clouded over here, and the air was a little bumpy with wind. They sailed out of the canyon, and suddenly there were houses below them, and roads, and cars. They were in a huge canyon, where the mountains reached the sea. The sea came partway into the canyon and formed a small bay. Many small fishing boats and a coastal freighter sat like ducks on the sheltered waters of the bay. The city of Seward was laid out in neat rows of buildings on the narrow, flat shelf of land that reached to the edge of the blue, deep water of the bay.

"Seward! Clang! Clang! Seward!" shouted Tex Doan. "Say, Will, I never did learn how to land this here airplane, so I'll just come in low and you jump. Okay?"

"Okay, Tex. Say when," laughed Mr. Brinkman.

Tex Doan dived the plane at a building and pulled up, gunning the engine. Blue-John's stomach felt like it flopped over.

Tex Doan banked the plane around and buzzed the building again. As he came around again a person came out of the building and waved. The person ran to an ambulance parked near the building.

"They got the signal," said Tex Doan. "That guy with the ambulance will meet us at the airport to get y'all, Will, so let's see if we can beat him to the airport."

In a moment they had landed, and, as they were taxiing to a parking place, the ambulance raced onto the field.

"An hour and three minutes, I make it," said Tex Doan, checking his watch. He shut off the engine. "Sure beats walking."

The ambulance pulled alongside the plane and they all got in and rode to the hospital. At the hospital a doctor examined Mr. Brinkman's cut, swollen foot.

"Well, Mr. Brinkman," said the doctor when he had finished the examination. "You're a lucky man. It could have been much more serious. You have a severe laceration, and some tendons cut, but there is no bone damage that I can find."

Blue-John's stepfather was much relieved. "That's the best news I've had in a month."

"The major concern here is infection," continued the doctor. "However, the circumstances of the cut appear to have been fairly clean, so we may not have any problems there." He summoned a nurse. "And now, Mr. Brinkman, it's about time we sewed your foot back together."

Tex Doan put his hand on Blue-John's shoulder. "Well, Towhead, looks like your daddy's in good hands. Guess we might as well head on back to Soldotna." He saw Blue-John was reluctant to leave. "There ain't really nothing more we can do. And your mama needs y'all on the homestead."

Mr. Brinkman took Blue-John by the arm. "You help take care of things, John. And be extra careful with that bear around. Latch everything up tight at night. Be *sure* you latch the barn door at night after Molly has her calf." He frowned. "John, I'd just rather you and your mother didn't go out in the hayfield to get the rest of the hay. Your uncle Kirk can bring his family over to help and you all can finish that field in a day." He was lying on an examination table, propped up on one elbow. He leaned toward his stepson. "We'll just have to take a chance with Ginger, out in the pasture. We can't keep her cooped up in the barn with Molly." He ruffled Blue-John's hair. "But we're *not* going to take a chance with you, or your mother, or Angie. Okay?"

86

Blue-John grinned. "Okay, Dad. Hope you're feeling better soon. I'll take in the tractor and wagon on the way home today." He hesitated. "Well, that is, if I can get it started."

His stepfather winked. "You'll get it started." Blue-John knew his stepfather had not mentioned the incident in the field to Tex Doan.

"And I'm pretty sure I can start the generator. We'll get along fine. Hope you're feeling better soon."

"Oh, I'll be out in a few days. Right, Doctor?"

"More likely a week," replied the doctor.

Tex Doan broke in. "Well, if y'all aim to lay a-round here that long, I'll just fly the whole herd of them over to visit in a couple of days. Christine and me can ride in front and little Angie in back. Juanito, here, can sit on the wing." He stuck out his hand. "Be seeing y'all, Will."

"Thanks for the plane ride, Tex," said Mr. Brinkman.

"Wait'll you see the bill!" They both laughed. Tex Doan led Blue-John to the door.

"So long, Dad," said Blue-John.

"See you later, John. Kiss your mother and Angie for me." He lay back.

Tex Doan and Blue-John went out to the ambulance to wait for a ride back to the airport.

"Your daddy's got grit," commented Tex Doan. "That foot must hurt something fierce, but he never said a word about it on the trip over."

Blue-John felt a surge of pride in his stepfather. "Yeah. He's okay."

The driver came out and they got in the ambulance. As they were riding out to the airport Tex Doan said, "So y'all got a grizzly on your place, huh? That's what your daddy said."

"We sure have! A big old bruiser! Boy, he's got feet like bushel baskets!"

"And claws like meathooks and a real mean temper, boy! How long has he been around your place?" asked Tex Doan.

"Couple days, I guess," replied Blue-John.

"What's he been doing? Has he bothered anything?"

Blue-John hesitated. "Well . . . not really. He seems to be just walking around, sort of looking."

"That won't last long," commented Tex Doan, spitting out the window. "And when he stops looking and starts doing, y'all got trouble. Big trouble. I'll drop over whenever I can and help y'all with chores. I carry a rifle in the truck, force of habit. Maybe I'll get a shot."

"Oh, you don't need to bring a rifle. He'll go

away." Blue-John looked up hopefully at Tex Doan. "Won't he?"

"Ain't likely, Sugarfoot. I'll fetch the rifle."

Blue-John didn't answer.

He was quiet on the flight from Seward back to Soldotna. He rode in the front and Tex let him hold the control briefly, but Blue-John couldn't get very enthusiastic. He seemed to be thinking about something else.

The sun was still two hours high when the yellow plane touched down on Tex Doan's flight strip. As they walked to the Doan house Mrs. Doan stepped out to meet them. "Well," she called, "there's Bowlegged Buzzard and Little Eagle. How was the trip? How's Will's foot?"

"Aw, hush up, you homely old critter," growled Tex Doan as he and Blue-John went to his truck. "I'm going to fetch the boy home. Tell y'all when I get back." They got in the truck. "Sure missed you on the trip, Honeypot." He spat a long stream of tobacco juice. "Yep, sure was quiet." He laughed, cackling like a bird, and started the truck. They roared out of the driveway and headed down the lane toward the Brinkman homestead.

As they were passing the hayfield Blue-John noticed the tractor and wagon. "Hey, Mister Doan, stop!" he shouted suddenly. "Let me out and I'll drive the tractor and wagon home."

"Oh? The tractor?" Tex Doan slowed down and looked where Blue-John was pointing. "Well, sure thing. Y'all can drive it okay?"

"Sure," answered Blue-John. Tex Doan stopped the truck and Blue-John got out.

"I'll go on and tell your mama what the doc said about your daddy's foot. Y'all can figure on flying over to Seward again in a couple of days." He waved and drove on.

"Thanks," called Blue-John, and he walked across the hayfield to the tractor.

There was still blood on the hitch and on the ground, and he stepped back. He hesitated, suddenly trembly and nervous. Then, carefully stepping over the blood, he climbed up on the tractor. He gripped the wheel. His hands felt sweaty. His foot trembled on the clutch. He turned on the switch and pushed the starter.

The tractor started instantly, roaring to life.

Blue-John leaned back and let out a big breath of air. He let the engine warm up, just to be sure. After a moment he carefully let out the clutch and backed up the tractor. Slowly he inched it back to the wagon, put it in neutral, and got down and dropped the pin into the hitch, hooking on the wagon.

He climbed on the tractor and put it in gear. He swallowed hard, gripped the steering wheel with both hands, and let out the clutch.

The tractor started smoothly down the field. Blue-John looked back and checked the wagon following him.

He faced ahead. The wind in his face was cool. He was grinning.

He sailed down the field, straddling a windrow, looking now and then at the woods on the far side of the field slowly slipping past.

Then he saw the bear.

It broke suddenly from the woods and began running in the same direction as Blue-John, along the edge of the woods. The bear didn't look at Blue-John. It seemed to be chasing something. Suddenly it whirled and went crashing into the woods. A moment later Blue-John saw what the bear had been chasing.

A young cow moose staggered from the woods a little farther on. Its neck and side were red with blood. The moose staggered a short distance into the hayfield, and stood teetering on wobbly legs. It couldn't seem to hold up its head.

Suddenly the bear burst from the woods and headed straight for the moose. The moose tried to run, but it was too late. With a chilling roar the bear caught up with the moose and struck it a bone-snapping blow in the neck. The moose was knocked flat. Still roaring, the bear leaped upon the fallen moose.

Blue-John stared.

The tractor veered off course and he jerked the steering wheel to straighten it out. He gave the tractor more gas and roared down the field toward the barn lot.

He slowed down to make the turn between the tractor shed and the barn. In his excitement he couldn't remember how to use the two separate brakes on the tractor until he had almost reached the house. Finally he got the tractor stopped, in the driveway.

He shut off the tractor and jumped down.

Mrs. Brinkman rushed from the house to meet him.

"Mom! The bear . . . !" Blue-John started to say.

His mother interrupted. "Thank heavens you're home, John. I went out to milk Ginger after Tex Doan left, and . . ." She shoved him toward the house. "Well, see if you can start that cranky generator. I think Molly's about to have her calf!" She hurried on to the barn.

Blue-John stood staring after her, then he went into the house.

Angie was in the kitchen, sharing a cookie with Burrs. Blue-John flopped down in a chair. He rubbed his head for a moment. Then he looked at Angie. "Hey!" he said. "I went up in an airplane. Dad's foot is going to be all right. I drove the truck. I drove the tractor. The bear caught a moose. And Molly's about to have a *calf*!"

He leaped to his feet and kicked playfully at Angie.

"WHOOEEE!" he yelled, and ran out to start the generator.

CHAPTER SEVEN

The Calf

BLUE-JOHN dashed around the house to the generator lean-to. He paused, and glanced at the barn, then jerked open the door to the lean-to and went inside. He flipped on the diesel engine's ignition switch and pulled the choke knob out. He had seen his stepfather do this. He pressed the starter button.

The starter whined. The engine wouldn't start. For several minutes he worked with the engine, trying to start it. Finally, frustrated, he yelled, "Stubborn old clunker!", shut off the switch and ran to the barn.

His mother was standing at Molly's stall, looking inside.

Blue-John ran to the stall and peered inside. Molly was lying in some hay that Mrs. Brinkman had scattered

94

in the stall. The cow seemed to be breathing hard. "Anything yet?" asked Blue-John, breathless.

"Nothing yet," answered his mother. She pointed to an electric light bulb hanging above the stall. "Couldn't get the diesel started, I see."

"Naw," scowled Blue-John. "I think there's some dealybob I didn't push or pull on the old thing. I mean, I think Dad always did more than just pull out the choke, only I can't remember just what. Maybe I'll think of it." He stood watching Molly.

"Well, I hope you do. I'd rather not have to use lanterns tonight." She started to leave the barn. "Doesn't look like Molly's quite ready. I'll go get something started for supper."

Blue-John remained at the stall. "I'll be in pretty soon," he said.

"Okay," called his mother as she went out.

Blue-John turned to the cow. For a long time he looked at her. Finally he said, "Well, old Molly, so you're going to have your calf tonight, huh? Well, just remember what I told you. You better have a girl. If you have a boy they'll eat him. Remember now."

He left the barn and went to the house. In the kitchen his mother was getting supper ready. "I didn't have time to take care of the rabbits, John. Would you do it?"

"Uh, well, sure, if you think there's time."

Mrs. Brinkman emptied a package of macaroni into a pan on the stove. "Time?" she asked.

"Yeah. You know, the calf might—well—"

"John, I'm sure there's time," smiled his mother.

"Well, okay," agreed Blue-John, not convinced. He went out, and trotted around the house to the rabbit hutches. There were four hutches lined up against the wall of the chicken house, four wooden boxes with wire fronts and a smaller wooden box in each one, where each rabbit could huddle in comfort against the winter cold.

From cabinets under the hutches Blue-John quickly got scoops of green pellets and rationed out portions to each rabbit. There were two white rabbits, a gray one, and a speckled black and white one. He ran to the well, got a bucket of water, and ladled water to each rabbit. In his hurry he scattered pellets, spilled water, and left the cabinet doors open.

He threw the dipper at the well and raced to the barn. He dashed inside and peered into the stall where Molly lay. She looked at him calmly.

He trudged out of the barn. On the way to the house he closed the cabinet doors and hung the dipper on the well. When he went into the kitchen his mother asked, "No little one yet?"

Blue-John sat down. "Naw," he answered gloomily.

"Well, give the old girl time. She doesn't want to be hurried." She went on getting supper ready. "Isn't it wonderful that your dad's foot is not as bad as we thought. It looked horrible, with all that blood." She put bread on the table, and mossberry jelly. "Tex Doan suggested we all fly over and visit your dad tomorrow afternoon."

Blue-John looked up absently. "Oh yeah." He brightened. "Say, that would be swell!"

"Is it fun to go up in a airplane?" asked Angie.

"It sure is," he answered. "Boy, it is."

"Ain't it scary?"

"Naw."

"You weren't never scared? Ever?" Angie persisted.

"Well, for crying in a washtub! I said I wasn't, didn't I?" blurted Blue-John. "Probably little kids like you would be scared out of your old skin. I just sat there like I was—"

Angie interrupted. "How high up did you go?"

Blue-John scratched his head. "Well, I don't exactly know. Pretty high, I guess."

"Ten hundred?" asked Angie.

"Ten hundred what?"

Angie rubbed her nose. "Just ten hundred." She smiled brightly. "Ten hundred miles?"

Blue-John snorted. "Oh *boy*! Some smart sister I got!"

Mrs. Brinkman interrupted. "Now, John. She doesn't know her numbers yet. She's just starting first grade this fall." She grated cheese for the macaroni. "Your father will be out of the hospital the first of the week."

"Yeah," agreed Blue-John. "It sure was lucky the ax didn't cut any bones."

"Will they take good care of Daddy in the hospital?" asked Angie.

"The very best," answered her mother.

"And make his foot not hurt?"

"Yes, Sweetie, and make his foot not hurt."

Blue-John was nervously looking out a window at the barn.

"Could you see birds from up in the air?" persisted Angie.

"Well, sure," grumbled Blue-John. He started for the door.

"And cars and people and my cousin Mary Lou's house in Kenai?"

"John," called Mrs. Brinkman as Blue-John went out of the house. "Would you feed and water the chickens, and gather the eggs?" She went to the kitchen door. "And see if you can do something with that generator, will you?"

"Mama," asked Angie, "when we fly over to see Daddy will we fly over the sun?"

Blue-John raced to the barn. In a moment he came walking back. He stopped at the chicken coop and opened the door to a small storage room in one end of the little building. There were sacks of grain and feed in the storage room. He put scoops of each kind in troughs in the chicken coop. Then he carried a bucket of water from the well and filled a round water trough in the chicken coop.

He went back to the porch and got a basket, and went back toward the chicken coop. On the way he stopped suddenly, and looked toward the hay-field. The sun had slipped down behind the trees, leaving the sky a brilliant orange-pink. Shadows were growing darker in the deep woods, and reached far into the hayfield. He could see a hump of brown in the shadows in the hayfield. For a moment he studied the brown hump. It was hard to see it clear-ly in the shadows.

Abruptly, he whirled and ran back to the house, dropping the basket.

"Mom, I gotta use Dad's binoculars, okay?" he shouted as he dashed into the kitchen.

"What's happening?" Mrs. Brinkman asked. "In-dians coming?"

"Naw. I just thought of something! I started to tell you when I got home from the trip with Dad and you were busy and then I got busy and forgot and now I just remembered! Please, Mom. Bring the binoculars and come see! Now! It won't take but a minute!"

Mrs. Brinkman was startled. "Well, for heaven's sake, it sounds important. I guess the macaroni can cook by itself for a minute." She got a pair of binoculars from a case hanging on a gun rack in the living room. "Come on, Angie. We must see this."

Blue-John led them toward the barn. In the yard Mrs. Brinkman saw the empty egg basket. "Hmm," she commented. "The hens didn't earn their keep today?" She grinned. "Shame on them."

"Aw, I'll gather the eggs after I show you something," said Blue-John.

"Sure," laughed his mother. "Have you remembered how to start the engine for the generator?"

"Not yet," growled Blue-John as they reached the barn. "I need to study the old thing and figure it out. Did it start at all, when you tried it?"

"It started and ran for a few seconds, and then quit," replied Mrs. Brinkman.

Blue-John started up the ladder to the hayloft. "Hey! by golly! I remember!" He jumped down and excitedly started explaining to his mother. "Y'see, Dad wanted to be able to take off the fuel tank and clean it once in a while, so he put a valve in the fuel line where it fastened to the tank. When he wanted to clean the tank he could just shut off the valve and whip off the tank and clean it, and not bother anything else." He slapped the side of the barn. "Now *why* didn't I think of that before?"

He started toward the house, waving his arm. "Why, of course! Just a dumb old valve to open!"

"But John," called his mother, "aren't you going to show us something with the binoculars? You know, since we're already here?"

Blue-John whirled around and came back. "Aw, of course." He started up the ladder to the hayloft again.

"Gee, you sure forget a lot," teased Angie.

"He has a lot of things to think about, now that Daddy's in the hospital," said Mrs. Brinkman.

Blue-John waited at the top of the ladder and reached down to help his mother, and then Angie, up into the loft. He went to the hayloft door. He took the binoculars and began looking through them toward the hayfield.

"There! There he is! By golly, he's still there!" he shouted excitedly.

"Who is there?" asked his mother.

Blue-John gave the glasses to his mother and pointed. "There! Just see for yourself." He stepped back and put his hands on his hips.

"John!" gasped Mrs. Brinkman. "It's a bear!"

"It sure is!" he answered. "It's *the* bear. That old king bear that's been wandering around here."

Mrs. Brinkman continued to look. "He's eating something. A moose! I think he's eating a moose!"

"He sure is. I was driving the tractor and wagon in and saw the bear run down the moose. Boy, he hit that moose like a truck!"

Mrs. Brinkman lowered the binoculars and looked at Blue-John. "But John, don't you feel—sorry for the moose?"

"Well, sure," he said sadly. "I'm sorry for the poor moose. I'm sorry about anything that bear has to kill to eat. But it's gotta eat something, and I just guess we have more moose . . ." He looked down, and kicked some loose hay out the door. "Well, it's just that we have lots of moose around here, and only one bear like that one."

Mrs. Brinkman put her hand on Blue-John's arm. "Yes, Honey, and there's only one Molly, and one Ginger." She paused, looking at him. "And only one Angie, and one of your dad, and one of you, and one of me. And when that bear can't catch any more moose he's going to look for something easier to catch."

Blue-John stared in silence at the hayfield.

"You just don't believe that, do you, John?" asked Mrs. Brinkman.

Blue-John stuck his hands in his pockets. "I guess not."

"Well, Sugar, I hope the bear never proves it," commented Mrs. Brinkman softly, looking out at the hayfield.

Blue-John suddenly strode over to the ladder. "Guess I better start the generator." He went down the ladder.

Angie took the binoculars and peered through them at the big white rooster in the yard. "Why does John look that way?" she asked. "Like he's got a stomach-ache. Is he sick?"

Mrs. Brinkman watched Blue-John disappear into the generator lean-to. "I suppose you might say he has an ache, Angie, but it's not a stomachache." She took the binoculars. "Let's go see how that macaroni is doing, shall we?"

They went down the ladder. As they crossed the yard they heard the diesel engine roar to life, and by the time they entered the kitchen, the lights came on. In a moment Blue-John came into the kitchen, carrying the basket with some eggs in it. He put the basket on the kitchen counter.

"We checked on Molly when we left the barn," commented Mrs. Brinkman. "If we watch her so close she just might decide not to have the calf at all."

"How could she do that?" asked Angie. "Is it like company coming? How could she tell it not to come?"

Blue-John glared at his sister. He started to comment, but Mrs. Brinkman interrupted. "Supper is almost ready, kids. Why don't you wash your hands, Angie?"

Angie looked at her hands. "They isn't dirty. Look." She held them out.

Mrs. Brinkman looked closely at the small hands. "Hmm. Look at all those bacterianitsis crawling around." She put her hand to her mouth and gasped. "Oh! And thumblefinger germs and hoppaskippinotis bugs! You'd best wash them off quick or they'll carry off the silverware!"

Angie stared at her mother and then at her hands and then at her mother. "Oh, Mama, I don't see any—whatever you said." She grinned, and ran to the bathroom to wash.

Mrs. Brinkman put plates and glasses on the table. "Let's hope Molly has her little one before you kids go to bed."

"Won't we stay up with her, anyway?" asked Blue-John, surprised.

"Oh, you might, but Angie is too young to stay up all night. She would be just too tired to fly to Seward tomorrow to see your dad." She gazed out at the shadows stretching across the hayfield. "I can't help thinking he's about to come driving that tractor up from the hayfield."

Angie came back from the bathroom. She held out her hands. "See! No skippinjumpin bugs!" She sat down at the table.

"Good!" exclaimed Mrs. Brinkman. "Okay, John, your turn."

Blue-John washed, and sat down. "Chow down, Troops," sang out Mrs. Brinkman, and she dished out macaroni all around. They ate. Blue-John gulped down his supper in silence and finished early. He jumped up, saying, apologetically, "You know, Molly might . . . ?"

"All right," laughed his mother. He dashed out. Soon he was back. "Well, criminy, I wish she would hurry." He sat down and rested his head on his hand.

Mrs. Brinkman was clearing away the supper dishes.

Angie looked puzzled. "Mama," she asked, "where is Molly going to get her calf?"

Mrs. Brinkman and Blue-John looked at Angie, then at each other. "Why, it's inside her, Sugar. I guess I thought you knew that."

"No. I thought maybe the calf came from a store, or someplace." Angie thought for a minute. "How did it get there? Did God put it there?"

Mrs. Brinkman began washing the dishes. "Well, yes, He did, Honey, in a way."

"Well—why does the calf have to come from Molly, instead of some other cow?"

Blue-John interrupted. "Well, for crying out loud! So it will look like Molly, and be *her* calf. My gosh!"

"Oh, John, don't yell at me. You just don't know everything, I bet," scowled Angie. "Gee, I bet it's dark in there, where the calf is, huh?"

Blue-John got up. "John, for heaven's sake!" cried Mrs. Brinkman. "You know what I forgot?" She grabbed the milk bucket and shoved it into Blue-John's hand "I clean forgot to milk Ginger. I got so excited about Molly I forgot! Would you go out and milk the poor old girl, before she bursts?"

"Migosh! Sure." Blue-John dashed out.

Mrs. Brinkman was finishing the dishes. She was wiping the counter when Blue-John came tearing across the yard, yelling. He burst into the kitchen.

"Mom! Hey! It's here! The calf is here! Come quick!"

"Wonderful!" cried Mrs. Brinkman. She grabbed Angie's hand and they all dashed out of the kitchen. As they ran to the barn Blue-John tried to explain. "I looked, of course, when I first got to the barn. Then, I was just sitting there, milking Ginger—just *sitting* there, milking Ginger—and—and suddenly I heard this funny sound, and—I ran over to look, and—"

They ran inside the barn and looked in the stall.

"—and there it *was*!"

A tiny black and white calf lay wet and glistening in the hay. Molly calmly studied the three excited faces watching her calf.

"Just look at it, will you! Boy, that's the best calf around *anywhere*!" yelled Blue-John.

Mrs. Brinkman went into the stall with a pitchfork and raked up some fresh hay. She came out of the stall.

"It's a nice one, Blue-John. It's a real nice calf," she said.

"I'll bet it's glad it's not in the dark any more," commented Angie.

Outside, in the darkness of the hayfield, the bear had raked hay over the remains of the moose, and had gone into the woods to sleep.

CHAPTER EIGHT

To Bury a Moose

I T was early morning. A small owl sailed on sound-less wings into the hayloft. It perched on the frame of a ventilating window, and closed its great, yellow eyes. It slept, digesting the mice it had caught the night before.

Blue-John stood outside Molly's stall, watching the calf. The little calf was nuzzling Molly, getting its breakfast, and vigorously wagging its tail with satisfaction.

"Well, I'm glad you took my advice and had a girl, Molly," commented Blue-John. "Sure glad we don't have to eat him. And in a couple of years we'll get more milk, and have more calves. . . ." He paused, and frowned. "Sure sounds like a lot of work, putting up all that hay we'll need, and cleaning stalls and everything."

Finally the calf stopped feeding. It stared curiously at Blue-John. "I just guess maybe I'll name you Tuesday, huh?" said Blue-John to the calf. The calf whirled around and pranced across the stall, bobbing on unsteady legs. It ran into the hayrack.

"You can't drive no better than I can," laughed Blue-John. The calf lay down under the hayrack, curling up like a deer.

Blue-John climbed to the hayloft. He gazed into the hayfield for a long time. As he turned to go he looked up and saw the owl on the ventilating window. He tiptoed softly across the barn floor and started to climb the hay piled against the wall under the window. All the way he kept his eyes on the owl. The hay was slippery and he made a noise. The owl opened its eyes. Blue-John froze, and closed his eyes down to slits. He remained unmoving, watching the owl. The owl watched him. After a while Blue-John slowly eased back down and softly walked to the ladder. "Aw, well, I already got an owl." He started down the ladder but stopped to look back at the owl. "Just keep your mitts off the mice in the oat bundles," he growled. He went to the house.

"Just in time, Cattleman," called his mother as he went into the kitchen. "Breakfast is just about ready. Better wash your hands."

Blue-John stared out the window. "I wonder where

that old bear is right now," he said absently. "I'm sure glad he got himself something to eat." He paused. "There's an owl in the hayloft. A little one. I sure would like to catch a horned owl. Boy!"

"What on *earth* would you do with a great horned owl, John?" cried his mother.

"Oh, just keep it, I guess," replied Blue-John.

"I know, like you want to keep that ornery old bear out there," commented Mrs. Brinkman, putting dishes and silverware on the table. "Here. Since you're just standing there, set the table."

"Aw, I better wash my hands first," he muttered, ducking out of the kitchen. "Seems like I'm always washing my hands!" The bathroom door slammed shut.

"Angie! Hurry up, Honey. Breakfast," called Mrs. Brinkman. In a moment Angie came out, wearing one shoe.

"Where's your other shoe?" asked Mrs. Brinkman.

"I don't know," murmured Angie sleepily. "I thought they was in the living room, but I don't find one. Losted, I guess."

Her mother glanced toward the living room. "Oh, I'll bet it isn't lost, Honey." Angie sat down. In a moment Blue-John came in and sat down. Mrs. Brinkman put a plate stacked high with pancakes on the table. She said quietly, "Angie lost her shoe, John. Where do you suppose it is?"

He reached for the plate of pancakes, but his mother lifted it away from him. "Hmmm?" she smiled.

Blue-John grinned. "Aw, it's in the bathroom. But it's wet. I accidentally dropped it in the . . ."

"JOHN!" screamed Angie. She jumped up and started out. There was a thump as a shoe dropped to the floor. Angie came back slowly and peered under the table. Blue-John looked down.

"For crying out loud!" he cried. "There's your dumb old shoe, there! How'd it ever get there?"

"Oh, *you*!" cried Angie. "You make me so *mad*! You're the worstest brother I ever had!"

Blue-John laughed. Angie put on the shoe and they ate breakfast.

"Eat up, kids," urged Mrs. Brinkman. "We have a lot to do. I'll drive over to Tex Doan's right after breakfast and ask him if he'll come over and bury that moose. Then—"

"Bury the moose!" interrupted Blue-John.

"Certainly, bury the moose," replied his mother. "We can't have a dead moose rotting in our hayfield."

"But, the bear's eating it!"

"That may take awhile. Meanwhile, we can't get the hay, because of the bear."

"But, what will the bear eat, for crying out loud?" cried Blue-John.

"He'll have to go somewhere else, John. Maybe he'll go back into the bush, where he belongs. Then we can get the hay into the barn before it rains. And somehow, we've got to reach your uncle Kirk and get him to come help with the haying."

Blue-John grumbled, "Well, that's just great. The old bear finally gets himself a moose to eat and you're going to bury it."

"John!" commanded Mrs. Brinkman sharply. "Now, that's enough. We live here. We cannot share our farm with a grizzly bear."

They finished breakfast. As Mrs. Brinkman got up she said, "I'll take Angie and drive over to Tex Doan and ask him to come down and bury that moose before he flies us to Seward to visit your dad." Quickly she gathered up the breakfast dishes and put them in the sink. "The favors we ask that man!" She put a jacket on Angie, and got one for herself. "Better throw down some hay for the cows, John, and check the chickens and rabbits. I'll go to your uncle Kirk's in Kenai after I see Tex Doan. Maybe Kirk can come out this afternoon and help with the haying."

She started out. "You and Tex can decide where to bury the moose. I'll be back as soon as I can. Tex wants to leave for Seward by ten o'clock."

"But I want to stay and watch them bury—" protested Angie.

Mrs. Brinkman interrupted. "Hush, Angie. Be careful, John, and watch out for the bear."

Blue-John stood looking gloomily out the window, his hands in his pockets. "Okay, Mom."

Mrs. Brinkman and Angie got into the pickup and drove away. Blue-John went outside and checked the rabbit hutches. He gave the rabbits some pellets and cleaned out the hutches. He was pouring some water for the chickens when he heard Tex Doan's bulldozer coming. He had just finished tossing down hay for Molly and Ginger when Tex Doan turned in the driveway on the clanking, snarling bulldozer, and drove to the barn lot.

Blue-John came slowly out of the barn as Tex Doan climbed down. Tex left the engine running, and the dozer chuffed and popped quietly.

"Howdy, there, Blue-haired Boy," called Tex Doan, walking over to Blue-John. "How's that calf-critter? Big enough to milk yet?" He clapped Blue-John on the shoulder.

"Swell! It sure eats a lot! And it runs into things. But it sure is pretty! Come and see it."

113

"You bet, young feller. I'd admire to see it, but let's hustle. We got lots to do this morning."

"Won't take but a minute," claimed Blue-John as they went into the barn.

In a moment they came out. "That little heifer is as pretty as a ribbon-bow, John. She'll make you a fine cow in a couple of years." He climbed aboard the dozer. "Come on. We'll go plant that moose-meat. Y'all got any ideas about where to bury it? How about I gouge out a keyhole just inside the woods? I ain't got time to cart the carcass very far."

Blue-John hesitated, gazing out at the hayfield. He looked down, and stuck his hands in his pockets.

"John," scowled Tex Doan, "don't y'all want the moose buried? Oh, come on now, boy. Y'all can't just let that carcass lay out there in your hayfield!"

Blue-John looked at him. "Why not? The bear's got to eat."

"Why, sure, it has, John. It can eat anything it wants to out there in the bush, but—well, this here is a homestead, boy, with people, and livestock, and—" He put his hand on a rifle in a case tied to the dozer. "The thing is, John, if it was my hayfield, I'd shoot the dad-burned bear and be done with it." He leaned down. "But your mama says 'No.' She says bury the moose and maybe that bearskin will take the hint and move on. Well, I don't think it'll

114

work. I'm betting the bear stays, even after we bury his moosemeat, and then y'all got a mad bear and that's real trouble." He paused, and jerked his thumb toward the hayfield. "Come on and help me."

Blue-John shook his head.

Tex Doan gunned the engine and the dozer went roaring and clanking out of the barn lot.

Blue-John stood with his hands in his pockets and watched the dozer crawl slowly down the hayfield toward the dead moose.

Finally, without moving, he cried out, "Do people always have to win? DO PEOPLE ALWAYS HAVE TO WIN?"

Tex Doan clanked down the hayfield to the moose, and angled over to the woods. At the edge of the woods he scraped a bare spot in an opening in the trees, and gouged out a shallow hole. He walked the snarling dozer back to the moose, lowered the blade, and tied the carcass of the moose to the front of the blade. Raising the blade, he clanked back to the hole and dropped the blade in the hole. He untied the moose, backed out the dozer, and shoved the dirt back in the hole, on the moose.

He clanked out of the hayfield. As he passed the barn he looked up. Through the big loft door he could see Blue-John, sitting in the ventilating window in the north end of the loft.

Blue-John sat with his knees drawn up. The owl was perched above the window, asleep. In the silence of the loft, the mice squeaked daintily in the oat bundles, and the hay in Molly's stall crunched as the new calf romped back and forth.

Blue-John looked out across the long meadow that stretched north of the homestead. It had been woods when the Brinkmans moved onto the homestead. Mr. Brinkman had dragged long, straight spruce logs from the woods with a tractor to build the barn. More of the tree trunks had been cut into lumber for the house and toolshed. Then Mr. Brinkman had used a chain saw, and rented Tex Doan's bulldozer, and had cleared off most of the trees, leaving a few to look pretty. The meadow was summer pasture for the cows.

At the far end of the meadow was a small log shack. It had been a trapper's cabin years ago. Abandoned and slowly crumbling, it leaned slightly from the weight of many winter snows. A brown, burly animal walked past the shack, and disappeared into some bushes.

"Him!" thought Blue-John, staring. "The bear!"

* * *

Mrs. Brinkman and Angie returned from Kenai in an hour, and shortly afterward they squeezed into Tex Doan's small plane and flew to Seward to

116

visit Mr. Brinkman. Early in the afternoon they returned. A station wagon was parked at the Brinkman
house. Two children ran from the barn as Mrs.
Brinkman parked her truck beside the station wagon.

Blue-John and Angie leaped from the truck and
ran to meet them. "Glen! Mary Lou!" they shouted.
The four children ran together in a collision of arms
and legs, thumping and slapping each other. A man,
and a woman holding a smaller girl by the hand
emerged from the barn.

"Chris! Hi Chris!" they called.

"Kirk! Dorothy! Well, this was good timing. How
long have you been here?"

"Oh, about twenty minutes," answered Mrs. Benteen. The little girl tugged at her hand, crying,
"Angie! Want Angie!" Mrs. Benteen let go of her
hand and the child immediately fell down. She
scrambled to her feet and ran after the other children, who were running to the barn.

"We been looking over your dairy herd, Chris,"
commented Kirk Benteen. "Nice-looking calf." He
was tall and lean, and wore denims. His hands were
sun-browned and muscular. His graying hair was
cropped short and his weathered face was craggy
and hawklike. His eyes were dark, and gentle.

"Yes, we're proud of it," answered Mrs. Brinkman.

"You are?" exclaimed Mrs. Benteen, acting surprised. "I thought Molly had the calf." They all laughed. "How was the trip to Seward? How is Will?"

"The air was a little bumpy down Resurrection Canyon," replied Mrs. Brinkman. "Will is in real good shape for a man with a gash in his foot. The doctor says he can come home in three days."

"Well, he got out of making hay," chuckled Mr. Benteen. "Chris, have you got some chores my fat wife could be doing? I'll take Glen and Blue-John and go rustle up some hay."

Mrs. Benteen aimed a playful kick at her husband. She, too, was tall, and had reddish-blond hair.

"Come on, Dorothy, we'll just sit in the house and drink coffee while they sweat in that hayfield." They went toward the house.

Mr. Benteen laughed and walked over to the tractor where Blue-John had managed to stop it the night before. He started it and swung it around to the barn. He parked the wagon under the loft door. "Hey, kids!" he yelled. "Let's pitch some hay!"

In a moment the four children came dashing out of the barn.

"Where's Alice?" Mr. Benteen asked.

"Looking at the calf," answered Glen, who was a freckled, red-haired boy of about thirteen.

"Let's toss this hay into the loft, boys." The girls whirled and dashed back into the barn. "I'll bet you haven't got enough pitchforks, Blue-John, have you?" commented Mr. Benteen as he got off the tractor.

"I'll look," replied Blue-John. He trotted into the barn and came back with one fork. "There's one in the loft and one still out in the field."

"Well, give me that fork and I'll toss the hay up. You and Glen take turns with the fork up in the loft." He climbed onto the wagon. "Throw the hay against the oat bundles to start."

He began pitching the hay from the wagon into the loft. Blue-John worked with the fork for a while. When he was tired he gave the pitchfork to his cousin and stood leaning against the side of the loft door.

Suddenly he straightened up, staring out across the hayfield.

"Hey!" he cried. "That's funny!"

Mr. Benteen stopped working and wiped sweat from his forehead. "What's funny?"

Blue-John paused. "Well, I thought Tex Doan buried that moose." He squinted against the sunlight. "But there's a brown thing laying in the hayfield that sure looks like a moose."

Mr. Benteen got off the wagon and climbed to the hayloft. He and Glen looked where Blue-John pointed.

"It looks like a moose, all right, John, but it's hard to tell from here," admitted Mr. Benteen, squinting. "Uh—tell you what, boys. You stay here, up in the loft. Keep your eyes peeled. If you spot that bear anywhere, leg it to the house and tell the women. Stay inside. I'll go out on the tractor to check on it, up close."

He climbed down, ran to his station wagon, and came back with a rifle. He unhooked the tractor from the wagon, started the tractor, and roared out of the barn lot.

Blue-John slid down the rope, bounced off the wagon, and dashed to the house. Soon he came running back with the binoculars. He climbed to the loft and studied the hayfield with the binoculars.

"Well," demanded Glen impatiently, "what's happening? What do you see?"

"Your dad ain't there yet."

"Can you see the moose?"

"Sure, and it's the one the bear killed. I can see where the bear was eating on it." He paused. "Your dad's almost there now."

"Let me see," demanded his cousin, grabbing the binoculars. "Yeah! There he is. He's circling around the moose. He's stopped to look at it—he's standing up, looking around. Boy, he's got that rifle ready—"

"Oh, no!" cried Blue-John. He grabbed the binoculars and they struggled briefly.

"Glen! Let go!" Blue-John sounded desperate, and Glen let go of the binoculars. Startled, he said, "Aw, don't worry. My dad's a good shot." Blue-John looked through the binoculars.

"Well," asked Glen. "Does he see the bear?"

Slowly Blue-John swung the binoculars as he scanned the edge of the forest. He lowered the binoculars. "No. He's coming back."

Glen took the binoculars. "Heck! I sure wish he could get a shot at that bear, don't you?" He moved the glasses around, looking at things.

Blue-John sat down on the hay. Then he lay back and put his arm over his face.

* * *

The sun was low in a scarlet western sky, searing the treetops, and the barn roof, and Blue-John's house with flaming color. From the woods dark shadows were reaching into the hayfield. From the woods came the sound of Tex Doan's bulldozer. It seemed to be raging and snarling, as Tex Doan worked to re-bury the mangled remains of the resurrected moose. The tractor was parked nearby. Kirk Benteen sat on the tractor, unmoving, watchful, his rifle ready.

"Yahooooo!" yelled Glen as he swung out of the hayloft door on the rope hanging from the barn peak. He dropped to the hay on the wagon, bounced off, and ran into the barn. His sister Mary Lou followed him down the rope, then Angie, and finally Blue-John.

They were having a hayloft race. They would swing out on the rope, drop into the hay on the wagon, scramble up the ladder, scuttle down the tunnel behind the oat bundles, squirm up through the hay under the ventilating window, slide down the hay and swing out on the rope to start all over again.

Laughing, squealing, screaming, around and around they went, till their hair was matted with hay, and then, damp with sweat and itchy with chaff they all piled up, exhausted, in a tangle of arms and legs, on the haywagon.

Finally Tex Doan came clanking into the barn lot on the dozer, followed by Kirk Benteen on the tractor. Mr. Benteen shut off the tractor. Both men climbed down.

"I never seen nothing like it, Kirk," said Tex Doan. "That bear brute just dusted the fill dirt off that moose and reached in the hole and hoisted out the moose like it was a bag of feathers." He shook his head.

"And lifted it straight up and out, from the looks of the marks around the hole," added Mr. Benteen. "And with sore teeth, maybe."

Tex Doan whistled softly. "That rightly is some all-fired bear. Strong? Why, if he was to take a notion, he might carry this whole barn over into the woods just so he could munch on the cows at his leisure."

"Why do you think he dragged the moose back into the hayfield, instead of just feeding on it in the woods?" asked Mr. Benteen.

The children had crowded around them now, listening.

"Just to show us he's still king of the mountain, I guess," answered Tex. He put his hands on his hips and squinted thoughtfully toward the woods where the moose was buried. "Y'know, Kirk, I got me a strange hunch about that bear, since it dug up that moose and dragged it back into the hayfield."

Kirk Benteen grinned. "You mean like it's going to come around tonight and bury your dozer?"

"Naw," laughed Tex Doan. "What I mean is, some years ago I had a neighbor, name of Rafferty. Him and his wife and brood tried to homestead down the road a piece."

"I know," nodded Kirk Benteen. "They finally went back to Ohio, or someplace."

"Michigan," corrected Tex Doan. "Well, sir, Rafferty told me once about a overgrown grizzly he almost locked horns with. Seems that a black bear on Rafferty's place had gotten real troublesome, scaring the livestock and eating Rafferty's rabbits. So Rafferty set out a big steel double-armed trap in a likely place, figuring to catch the black bear. Now, that trap was mean enough to bite your leg in half, or mine, if we was to step in it."

Kirk Benteen nodded. The children listened, wide-eyed.

Tex Doan spat a jet of tobacco juice and went on. "Well, now, next day he went to check that there trap. Something had been there, all right. Something had stepped in that trap, got real mad, and just made hash out of the trap." He paused. "And then walked off."

He spat again. "From the tracks all around, and some hair stuck to what was left of the trap, Rafferty figured it was a grizzly. One all-fired Texas-big grizzly."

"Gee," whispered Glen.

"Did he ever see the bear again?" asked Blue-John.

"Well, now, Boy-Who-Sits-In-Haylofts, he seen more of that bear than he had a mind to, that's for sure. A lot more. Just tracks at first, and diggings. Figured maybe that buster happened to stray this far from the river in the spring. Then, the next fall Rafferty was hunting moosemeat. Late in the afternoon he shot a cow moose right about where Will Brinkman's hayfield is now. 'Course, there was woods there then. He was just about to skin out the critter when all of a sudden there come a big grizzly, loping through the trees, right at him."

He spat and hitched up his pants. "Now, Rafferty just happened to have a little varmint-sized gun with him that day. Little 25–20 Winchester. He looked at that little 25–20 and he looked at that bear coming on and he done a real smart thing. He climbed a tree."

They all laughed nervously.

"Well, sir, that bear just trotted up to that moose like he owned it and started eating. Didn't even look at Rafferty. Bears usually like their dinner-meat old and moldy, but they ain't always choosey. So the bear just helped himself, real leisurely-like. Sure ruined that moosemeat."

"Where was Rafferty all that time?" asked Kirk Benteen.

Tex Doan howled and slapped his leg. "Up in the tree, of course!"

"Up in the tree?"

"Yep, up in the tree! He wasn't about to come down," cackled Tex Doan. "There was a hard frost that night, and Rafferty just sat there like a bird, shivering and cussing, and listening to the bear crunching bones and munching moosemeat."

They all roared with laughter.

"Sometime during the night the bear left, but Rafferty stayed in that tree till sunup, when he could see good." Tex Doan squinted again at the woods. "Thing is, Rafferty had plenty of time to study that dad-burned bear before dark. He noticed something strange about the bear." Tex held out a hand and tapped the back of it with a forefinger. "It had some little patches of dead white hair on the back of one front foot. Left one, I think. Like the hair or skin had been deadened once."

He paused. "Like, say—in a steel trap."

He walked to his bulldozer. "Rafferty never seen the bear again. Must have took off for other parts."

Kirk Benteen cleared his throat. "You think maybe this bear on Will's homestead is Rafferty's bear, come back?"

From the woods an owl called, softly, mournfully, in the stillness. A gas lantern blinked on, yellow-white, in Blue-John's home.

"Don't know, Kirk, don't know. Like I say, the bear digging up that moose and dragging it back into the hayfield set me to thinking. Just a hunch. If it was still alive it would be a pretty old bear, by now."

He spat a jet of tobacco juice into the darkness. "Well, he ain't going to be king of the hill around here. This time I knocked him off his throne. I planted that moose five feet down, and packed it hard, and shoved trees over it. He won't dig it up again, and that's a guarantee!"

He suddenly turned and climbed aboard his dozer. "Well, I got to git. My war department is waiting supper on me. Say hello to your wife, Kirk. Glad to see you again. So long, kids." He waved and roared away, clicking and clanking.

"Well, kids," commented Mr. Benteen. "We didn't get much hay into the barn. And it looks like you stuffed most of it down your necks. We'll have to stay here tonight, and start early in the morning." He started toward the house. "I'll start the generator, Blue-John, while you and Glen lock up the barn."

The girls whooped and hollered and raced for the house. Blue-John and Glen closed the trapdoor to the haydrop and swung down on the rope. Blue-John started the tractor and pulled the wagon away from the barn so Glen could close and latch the main door. He shut off the tractor and sat for a moment, looking at the dark woods where the disputed moose was buried.

"Hey, John! You going to sleep on that tractor? Race you to the house. And I'll run backwards," taunted Glen. Blue-John leaped from the tractor to chase him.

Hours later that night, when all in the house were asleep, a deep, raging roar suddenly shook the woods where the moose was buried.

Moments later the bear charged out of the darkness into the circle of yellow brightness under the yard light. For a long time he stood, bold, bristling with rage, watching the darkened house.

Finally, abruptly, he turned and strode directly to the barn. He stepped slowly around the barn, nose high, testing the air, sorting out the scents of hay, and mice, and oats, and Ginger, and Molly, and a new scent, Tuesday. He stood for a moment, studying the barn.

Then he whirled, and padded off into the misty darkness.

CHAPTER NINE

Ambush at the Cabin

"OKAY, there, Johnny Blue-ears, move it on," called Kirk Benteen. Blue-John put the tractor in gear and pulled the wagon a short distance down the row of hay.

It was early morning. The three of them, Mr. Benteen, his son Glen, and Blue-John, had been making hay since soon after sunup. The dampness of the night had been burned away by the warm rising sun and they labored in a golden haze of sunlight. From the north a gray ceiling of clouds was sweeping slowly southward. In the distance the horizon was misty with rain.

Mr. Benteen squinted at the sky and studied the expanse of the hayfield. "Better shake a leg, boys," he commented. "It's going to get wet around here."

He and Glen pitched hay onto the wagon. In a moment he called, "Hey, Dreamer, we can go now!"

Startled, Blue-John jumped. He moved the tractor and wagon. He had been watching an eagle sweeping in wide circles against the sky. Two whiskered ravens followed the wagon briefly down the row. Mice occasionally scurried from the hay, frightened by the snarling tractor.

Mr. Benteen and Glen pitched hay onto the wagon until it was mounded high and round. Long streamers of hay trailed from the wagon, almost hiding the wheels. Mr. Benteen gave his fork to Glen and climbed onto the tractor. Glen climbed the wooden rack on the front of the wagon and stuck the forks in the top of the hay. Then he sprawled on the hay.

"Let's get this rolling haystack to the barn, John," said Mr. Benteen. They moved slowly toward the barn.

At the barn Blue-John pulled the wagon under the big loft door. Angie and Mary Lou suddenly poked their heads out the loft door and shouted, "Bang! Bang!" They squealed and ducked back inside.

Glen yelled, "Get the heck out of there, you silly girls!" He tossed one of the pitchforks into the loft. The top of the hay on the wagon was higher than the loft floor and he leaped into the loft. Squealing and giggling, the girls scrambled down the ladder.

Blue-John took turns with Glen, piling the hay in the loft as Mr. Benteen tossed it up from the wagon. Within an hour they had emptied the wagon. The loft was hazy with dust and chaff floating in the sunlight that flooded the loft. Sticky with sweat and itchy with chaff, the boys jumped down to the wagon. They ran to the well and drank and splashed water on each other while Mr. Benteen went to the house for a cup of coffee. The boys sneaked to the barn with tin cans of water and splashed Angie and Mary Lou, who were playing house in an empty stall. The girls screamed and the boys ran out of the barn, laughing.

The boys were sitting on the top rails of the hay-racks on the ends of the wagon when Mr. Benteen came out.

"Uncle Kirk," asked Blue-John, "can we drive down the edge of the field, near the woods, on the way out?"

"Sure, John," answered his uncle. "What's over there?"

Blue-John hesitated. "Oh, I thought maybe we could check on that moose. You know, see if the bear dug it up."

"No chance of that, John, but we'll check. Wouldn't take but a minute." Mr. Benteen walked quickly to his station wagon and returned with a rifle. He climbed on the tractor. He glanced at the boys perched on the racks on the ends of the wagon. "You boys stay up there. Hang on tight."

He started the tractor and drove out of the barn lot, and headed across the field toward the woods. As they drew near the woods he drove more slowly, and stood up, scanning the woods, rifle ready. At the place where the moose was buried he stopped the tractor, but left the engine running. Taking the rifle, he climbed onto the rack on the front of the wagon with Blue-John. For a long time he and the boys studied the woods.

"See anything moving?" asked Mr. Benteen quietly.

"No," answered Blue-John.

"Nothing," replied Glen.

"Stay here," commanded Mr. Benteen. He climbed down and walked softly into the woods, following a trail of bulldozer tracks. The boys could see him as he walked around and climbed over a jumble of dirt and tree trunks. In a moment he came out, and got on the tractor.

"The bear was there. It tried to dig out the moose again. It didn't have any luck. It couldn't move the trees. That bear has either moved on or it's one awful mad bear."

He started to move the tractor, and then stopped.

He stood up and looked toward the barn. "I wish I had told those girls to play in the house."

In the barn Angie and Mary Lou had gone up to the loft to play in the new hay.

Mr. Benteen and the boys, still riding the end-racks of the wagon, started across the field. Before they were halfway across the field a little girl's shrill, thin scream pierced the air.

Mr. Benteen stopped the tractor, stood up, and looked toward the barn.

A muffled roar came from the barn. There was another scream, so high and pure that it seemed to linger in the still air after it had stopped.

Mr. Benteen dropped into the seat and gunned the engine, just as the screams of two small girls merged in sheer terror. Blue-John and Glen climbed down and struggled to stay on the bouncing wagon as Mr. Benteen roared wide open down the field toward the barn. A gray curtain of rain met them as they careened toward the barn.

When they reached the barn Mr. Benteen yelled to the boys, "Stay where you are," and leaped from the tractor, rifle ready.

"Up here, Kirk!" called Mrs. Brinkman, who appeared in the loft door. Mr. Benteen clambered to the loft. Angie and Mary Lou were huddled near

133

the oat bundles, sobbing. Mrs. Benteen was comforting them. Mrs. Brinkman held the shotgun.

"We just got here," said Mrs. Brinkman, going back to the girls.

"What is it? What happened?" demanded Mr. Benteen, looking around.

"The bear," answered Mrs. Brinkman.

"Daddy!" cried Mary Lou, running to her father. Mr. Benteen picked her up and comforted her.

"What about the bear?" he asked. "Did the girls see him?"

"They saw him," answered Mrs. Benteen, still holding Angie. "They say he got the calf, Kirk."

Mr. Benteen stared at his wife in disbelief. "What!" he almost whispered. "He got the calf?"

"The girls are so shook up they haven't been able to tell us much yet, Kirk," Mrs. Benteen replied.

"We haven't gone back down, but there's blood outside the barn. You can see it from the door," added Angie's mother.

Mr. Benteen stepped to the loft door and looked down. There were splotches of bright red blood leading out of the barn and around the barn toward the garden. He climbed down and went to Molly's stall. Blue-John and Glen were there. Molly was standing against her hayrack, trembling and wild-eyed. Ginger was out in the meadow.

134

"He got your calf, John," said Mr. Benteen softly. Blue-John nodded. He stared in silence into the stall. Mr. Benteen put his hand on Blue-John's shoulder. After a moment he said, "We'll get him, John." He went back up to the loft.

"The girls say he just walked in the front door," said Mrs. Benteen. "He knocked down the door to the stall and stepped in and grabbed up the calf in his teeth and walked out. It was all so quick Molly didn't even have a chance to run out."

Mr. Benteen squatted down and took both girls in his arms. "Now, stop crying, Cupcakes. It's all right now. The bear is gone and he won't come back."

Mary Lou clutched her father. "Oh, Daddy, it was awful! We was laying on the floor, looking down at the calf in a big crack in the floor and—and the bear he walked in and mashed down the door and—" She began crying again. "It was awful."

Mr. Benteen glanced out at the gray rain falling steadily on the homestead. "Let's take the kids to the house," he said. He carried Mary Lou down the ladder and Mrs. Brinkman brought Angie.

"Better run the tractor into the shed, John," Mr. Benteen called. "Glen, close the car windows." They ran toward the house, and Glen dashed to the station wagon. Blue-John boarded the tractor. The engine was still running. He wheeled it around and drove the tractor into the tractor shed, leaving the wagon sticking out. For a moment he hesitated, then he dashed out into the rain.

He ran back into the barn.

He was sitting hunched up in the ventilating window when Ginger ambled into the barn through the small north door, and went to her stall. She pulled a mouthful of hay from the rack. The hay crunched and snapped as she slowly chewed it.

Blue-John sat without moving, staring into the rain. The rain was light, and fell quietly on the barn, and the cabbages, and the potatoes. A raven flew hastily from one side of the long north meadow to the other side. The rain was falling quietly on Blue-John's calf, Tuesday, somewhere in the dark woods beyond the meadow. Today was Thursday. The calf had lived two days.

Rain swirled against the window opening, and dampened Blue-John's pants leg. He didn't notice. Out there in the quiet gray rain, was the bear.

Softly Blue-John whispered, "You done it now. You done it now, you crazy, ornery old bear. You stubborn, tom-fool, stuck-up—STUBBORN OLD BEAR! Why didn't you give up? Why don't you give up now and go away? Why don't you just go away? They'll get you now. They'll get guns, now, and come after you. You can't win, old bear, you never could win!"

He cried softly.

The rain drummed softly on the tin roof.

"Hey, Blue-John!" Glen called from downstairs. "You in here? Where are you?"

Slowly Blue-John got down from the window and went to the haydrop. "Yeah?" he muttered.

Glen appeared at the ladder. "Your mom was worried about you. What are you doing up there?"

"Nothing," replied Blue-John as he climbed down the ladder.

Glen noticed Blue-John's reddened eyes. "Too bad about your calf. I'm sure sorry. Well, Dad's going to see if he can catch that bear."

"What?" cried Blue-John. "Already? I mean, well, it's raining."

"Oh, he's going to wear your dad's rain slicker. Mom doesn't want him to go, but he says something's got to be done about that bear, quick, before someone gets chewed up."

They peered out into the rain. At that moment Mr. Benteen came out of the house, carrying his rifle. He went north, through the garden, following the bear's tracks in the soft soil.

"Hey!" exclaimed Glen. "If we go up in the loft

we can watch him for a long way. Come on!" He and Blue-John scrambled up the ladder and watched through the ventilating window. "I bet that bear is laying up in the woods somewhere," said Glen. He sounded worried. "It would be hard to get a clear shot in there. The bear might jump Dad."

"Maybe your dad won't find the bear," suggested Blue-John, almost whispering. They watched for a moment. The figure of Mr. Benteen grew smaller and harder to see as he went further down the meadow.

"Sure is hard to see, in this rain," complained Glen.

Suddenly Blue-John whirled and slid down the hay. "I'll get the binoculars! Keep an eye on your dad." He raced out of the barn. In a moment he was back.

"Mom gave me an argument about maybe the bear would come back to the barn, but she knows he couldn't get up here," he said, breathless. "Where's your dad now?"

"Can't see him right now. I think he's down in that little gully at the end of the meadow. Give me the glasses, quick!" Glen took the binoculars and looked. After a moment he said, "Yes, there he is. He's going up out of the gully."

"You can't see the bear somewhere, can you?" asked Blue-John.

"Well, of course not, bird-brain!" snapped the older boy. "Dad would blast that bear if it was there." He continued looking. "Now he's getting near that old shack. He's going around some bushes. He's looking down at the ground, probably checking tracks." He handed the binoculars to Blue-John. "Want to watch?"

Blue-John shook his head, then changed his mind. "Aw, okay." He took the glasses and looked. Suddenly he stiffened, and sucked in his breath.

Glen looked over and said, "Yeah?"

"The bear! The bear!" cried Blue-John. "He charged out of the bushes and attacked your dad!"

"What!" screamed Glen.

"Your dad shoots—Oh, he's down. Your dad is down!—The bear is hit! He's spinning around! There's blood on the bear!—Your dad is trying to get up!"

Glen grabbed the binoculars. "Oh, Dad! Quick! Shoot! Shoot!—Oh, look out Dad! The bear! Here he comes! Get away! Get away!" Suddenly Glen was silent, watching through the binoculars. Almost without breathing, he watched, helplessly. Finally he lowered the binoculars and turned to Blue-John. "He made it. Dad made it to the shack," he said, looking at Blue-John. "He's hurt." He stared at Blue-John, unbelieving. "John, the bear almost got him! He's hurt!"

Without a word they whirled and raced to the ladder.

As they burst into the kitchen Glen shouted, "The bear got Dad! He's hurt!"

"Oh, no!" cried Mrs. Benteen. "What do you mean? What happened? Where is he?"

"In that old trapper's cabin. He got away from the bear." Quickly Glen and Blue-John told the women what happened.

"Where was the bear, Glen, after Kirk got inside the cabin?" asked Mrs. Brinkman anxiously. "What was it doing?"

"Running around the cabin. It's hurt, too. It was limping," answered Glen.

Mrs. Brinkman jerked a jacket from the coat rack and put it on. She tossed a jacket to Mrs. Benteen. "We've got to get Kirk out of that cabin."

"What about the bear?" asked Glen.

"Let's hope the tractor scares it away," answered Mrs. Brinkman grimly. She looked at Glen. "And just don't ask me what we'll do if the bear wants to fight it out. Get a blanket from a bedroom, Dorothy." She got a large oilcloth from a kitchen cabinet, and gave it to Glen. "Carry this, Glen, and you boys grab jackets. It's going to be wet out there."

Mrs. Benteen came back with a blanket. "We'll need the wagon. We couldn't all get on the tractor."

Mrs. Brinkman looked at Blue-John. "What do you think, John? Can you reach him with the tractor, pulling the wagon?"

"I'll sure try!"

Mrs. Brinkman got the shotgun from a closet and loaded it. "Can you get the wagon to the cabin, John?"

"I don't know. The ground is kind of wet and slippery. It might be hard to get across the gulley."

"Well," said Mrs. Brinkman, determined, "we'll do something when we get there." She leaned down to Angie and Mary Lou. "You girls will have to stay here by yourselves for a while. We have to go get Uncle Kirk. You watch the fort for us, okay?"

The girls nodded, wide-eyed.

"We'll be back soon. Now, there might be Indians or something outside, so after we leave, you lock the door and *stay inside*!"

Holding hands, the little girls nodded again.

"You girls are in charge, now, so take care of Alice."

They nodded again, and clutched Alice.

Mrs. Brinkman looked at Dorothy Benteen, then at Blue-John and Glen. "Well, let's go."

They went out, and dashed to the tractor shed. On the way, Mrs. Brinkman paused at the gas bottles to shut off the gas into the house.

She and Mrs. Benteen climbed onto the wagon and Blue-John and Glen boarded the tractor. Blue-John wheeled the tractor around and they roared out of the barn lot. Instead of following the bear's trail across the garden Blue-John took the wagon path down along the edge of the woods to the meadow. When he reached the meadow he opened the throttle. The speed drove the rain into their eyes, and ears, and down their necks. They were soon soaked to the skin.

At the gulley Blue-John stopped, and stood up. The cabin was on the other side of the gulley.

"What is it, John?" his mother called.

"I ain't sure we can get up the other side of the gulley, Mom. It looks awful slick."

"Could we push if it gets stuck?" asked Mrs. Benteen.

"We couldn't, Dorothy. The tractor's too heavy," replied Mrs. Brinkman.

They looked across the narrow erosion ditch to the trapper's cabin where Mr. Benteen lay inside, injured, perhaps dying.

"Mom!" called Blue-John, excitedly. He pointed up the gulley. "Maybe I can go down into the gulley here, where there ain't no rocks, and up the gulley to where the bank ain't so steep, and go out there." He paused, squinting against the rain. "We'd come out into some bushes. The bear might be waiting there. I don't see him around the cabin."

"We'll have to chance it, son," answered Mrs. Brinkman. She jumped down and ran to the tractor. "Glen, ride on the wagon with your mother. Sit down and hang on. I'll ride up here with the shot-gun." Glen got down and ran back to the wagon.

"Well, John, it's up to you," his mother said quietly.

Blue-John eased the tractor down into the gulley and turned sharply. He roared up the gulley, gaining speed. Water was trickling down the gulley. It sprayed from the wheels in muddy gray fountains. The tractor slithered crazily from side to side as Blue-John fought to keep it in the ditch. Suddenly he wrenched the steering wheel and the heavy machine shot up the bank of the gulley. The wheels sprayed mud as the straining, snarling tractor clawed its way out of the gulley.

They stormed up out of the gulley and smashed through the bushes. There was no bear. Blue-John slid the tractor to a stop at the door of the cabin.

"Stand guard, John," said Mrs. Brinkman, handing the shotgun to Blue-John. She and the others jumped down and ran to the cabin.

"Kirk! Kirk!" cried Mrs. Benteen. The door slowly opened. Kirk Benteen stood in the doorway, holding his rifle. His face was bruised and bleeding. Half of the rain slicker was ripped off and his shirt was torn open. He was holding a piece of the shirt against his bleeding shoulder.

He grinned weakly. "The Marines to the rescue," he said.

His wife hugged him, crying.

He looked admiringly at Blue-John, then at the gulley. "I could hear you coming up that chute. You're some driver, Blue-John." Soaking wet and splattered with mud, Blue-John grinned. Mr. Benteen looked toward the house. "I was going to try to walk out when I was sure the bear was gone." They helped him to the wagon. "Bear caught me by surprise. Real smart bear." They helped him onto the wagon. "Can't figure out how he didn't kill me in his first rush." He huddled against the endrack of the wagon, wrapped in the blanket and the oilcloth that shed the rain.

"You were lucky, Kirk," commented Mrs. Benteen fervently. "Thank heaven you were lucky."

"We'll look at these cuts when we get to the house. You may have to go to the hospital at Seward. Tex Doan could fly you over." Mrs. Brinkman looked up. "The sky is clearing."

Mr. Benteen shook his head in disgust. "I come

out to get the bear, and the bear gets me. And I wounded him, which was worse than not hitting him at all. He's raging mad, now."

Mrs. Benteen held the shirt bandage to his shoulder. Mrs. Brinkman fashioned a bandage for his head from a handkerchief. "It seems that I did this sort of thing just the other day," she commented quietly. "Let's go, John."

Glen rode the tractor, holding the shotgun. Blue-John wheeled the tractor around and headed for the gulley.

CHAPTER TEN

The Thunder of Rifles

I T had been nearly three hours since Tex Doan had lifted the yellow plane off his flight strip and roared toward Seward, carrying Kirk Benteen to the hospital. He would bring back Will Brinkman, if possible, who was urgently needed on the homestead now, with the wounded grizzly roaming the forest. Mr. Brinkman was not quite ready to leave the hospital, but Tex Doan hoped to get him released early.

Tex had hoped to make it back before dark, but if he didn't, Belle Doan would aim the truck headlights down the flight strip and Tex would use the plane's landing lights to land.

Mrs. Benteen had gone home with her three children, to finish the fishing season for Kirk. Glen had fished with his father, and knew how to work the net, and handle the boat.

The sun had long since slipped below the green wall of trees bordering the meadow beyond the barn. The western sky was still laced with fantails of fading red, but in the east the sky was growing dark. An immense, orange August moon was beginning to lift from behind the mountains into the clear, cool night air.

Somewhere a dog barked. Somewhere a great horned owl hooted solemnly. Somewhere in the darkening woods a great bear prowled, seething with rage, smashing small trees and ripping up patches of underbrush. Wounded, maddened, he gradually raged closer to the Brinkman homestead.

Blue-John stood in the big hayloft door, carefully searching with his eyes the hayfield, and the woods. Satisfied, he ran the length of the hayloft and scrambled up the opposite wall. At the top of the wall, near the peak of the sloping roof, was the small ventilation window. It was from this window that he saw his uncle Kirk being mauled by the bear. Now, he looked for the bear. Seeing nothing, he quickly slid down the hay, ran to the haydrop, and climbed down the ladder.

He picked up a bucket of milk in each hand and, leaning against the closed barn door, pushed it open.

He slipped through the doorway, set down the milk buckets, and closed the door and latched it. He picked up one bucket and hurried to the barn lot. He looked around the woods and meadow, then poured the bucket of milk into the barn lot. The milk was thick and yellow. It was Molly's milk, for her calf that lay broken and cold at the edge of the homestead. It was too rich for people to drink.

Blue-John picked up the bucket of Ginger's milk and headed for the house. He left both buckets at the well and trotted to the rabbit hutches. Looking around constantly, he fed and watered the rabbits, and then the chickens. The sky was growing darker and most of the chickens were in the coop, but two hens and the big rooster were still scavenging scraps in the yard. Blue-John circled around them, shooing them toward the coop. They dodged first one way and then another, avoiding him, but finally the two hens popped into the coop. The rooster darted past, and started to circle the yard again.

Furious, and becoming frantic, Blue-John lost his patience. He charged the rooster. Stiff-legged, the rooster waited to meet the boy in battle. At the last instant the bird lost its nerve and broke into a wing-flapping run. It streaked past the chicken coop. As it neared the barn it lumbered into the air and sailed up into the hayloft door and disappeared inside.

Blue-John rushed to close and latch the chicken coop door. He looked around, got the milk buckets, and hurried to the house.

His mother met him on the porch, the binoculars in one hand, and the double-barreled shotgun in the other. "He's nowhere in sight," she said. "I've been watching every foot of this place since you went out to milk, and he hasn't come out of the woods yet."

Blue-John put the milk inside the kitchen. "Maybe he won't."

Mrs. Brinkman gave him the binoculars and he put them in the kitchen. She shook her head. "He's wounded, and mad, John. And he figures we're the cause of all his trouble."

"I'll go start the generator now," said Blue-John sadly.

"I'll keep you company," replied his mother.

They went around the house and Mrs. Brinkman stood watching, outside the lean-to, while Blue-John went inside. "Don't waste any time, John," she cautioned. Her voice was quiet and calm.

"Don't worry, I won't," answered Blue-John's muffled voice from inside. The diesel starter whined. The engine fired, coughed, and died. The starter whined again. Nothing. Again the starter whined, and the engine sputtered and coughed and died.

Then Mrs. Brinkman, watching the north meadow,

gasped, and very softly, almost whispering, she said, "John. Let it go."

"Don't worry, Mom, I'll get it started in a minute," he answered, and the starter whined again.

Mrs. Brinkman's voice rose high and shrill above the whine of the starter. "JOHN!" The starter stopped. Blue-John poked his head out the door.

"Huh?" he asked.

She said quietly, "We haven't got a minute. Look!" She pointed with the shotgun.

Coming up the long meadow that stretched to the north of the homestead, was the bear. He was running at a trot, limping slightly, heading straight for the house.

Blue-John ducked back inside. The starter whined. "JOHN!" screamed Mrs. Brinkman. The starter whined again. "CHILD, LET IT GO!" screamed Mrs. Brinkman, and she reached inside and grabbed Blue-John. Just then the engine started. Blue-John adjusted it to an idle and leaped out of the lean-to. He slammed the door and they started around the house. Suddenly he stopped.

The engine had died.

They looked around. The bear was almost to the end of the meadow. He had almost reached the potato patch.

Mrs. Brinkman reached for Blue-John, but he

ducked away and darted back to the lean-to. "JOHN!"
Mrs. Brinkman ran after him.

"We got to have the light, Mom! We got to have
the light!" He jerked open the lean-to door and
ducked inside. The starter whined. The engine fired,
sputtered, and died.

The bear was coming through the potato patch.
He was roaring and snarling and snapping his teeth
together.

Mrs. Brinkman stood in front of the lean-to, fac-
ing the oncoming bear. She was holding the shotgun
loosely at arm's length. She was talking softly to
herself. "Will always said a big bear had to be almost coming down the gun barrel before you could
kill it with a shotgun." She took in a deep breath,
and let it out. "So I'll just wait, I guess, till he's close
enough."

The starter whined and the engine fired. Blue-John
revved it up. The roar of the engine shook the lean-
to. He let it idle.

The great bear had reached the garden, and was
charging through the cabbages, knocking off heads
of cabbage as he ran, head-high, proud, fearless,
roaring, bellowing his rage. His steel-hard muscles
were surging and driving under the rippling brown
fur, the terrible hooked claws tearing a channel of
destruction through the cabbages, the savage monarch

of the land, unafraid of death, charging his age-old enemy, to destroy or be destroyed. He broke into a dead run, thundering down on the small woman at the lean-to.

Mrs. Brinkman carefully lifted the shotgun to her shoulder.

Blue-John burst from the lean-to and slammed the door. "MOM! C'MON!"

They raced around the house and up onto the porch and into the kitchen. Mrs. Brinkman bolted the door, and stood the shotgun in a corner. They rushed to a window and looked out.

The bear charged into the yard between the house and the chicken coop and looked around. He was roaring and snapping his teeth. White foam rimmed his mouth. Cutting across one shoulder was a long, red gash, and his foreleg was smeared with blood.

"What is it, Mama?" asked Angie, who had come from her room. "What's out there?"

Mrs. Brinkman, startled, whirled around. She bent down and hugged Angie. "Little one, you might as well know. There's a bear out there, and he's . . . well . . ." She looked at Blue-John. "He's just—out there. And—we're in here." She stood up and brushed a strand of hair from her eyes. "And why don't I get some supper started, huh? I'll bet you're hungry as a b—"

She gasped, and leaned back against the counter. Her face was suddenly pale. She rubbed her cheeks with her hands. "I'll bet you're hungry—as a—" She leaned back and closed her eyes. "Go wash your hands, Angie, and don't argue with Mother, please."

Angie looked at her mother in alarm, and quietly left the room.

Blue-John came over and put his hand on his mother's arm. "Mom, are you all right?"

Mrs. Brinkman suddenly hugged Blue-John. "Sure, I'm all right. Just lost my grip for a minute." She straightened up, and quickly turned out the lights in the kitchen, and then in the living room.

"Why did you do that, Mom? It's nearly dark," asked Blue-John.

Mrs. Brinkman paused before she answered. She looked to see if Angie was coming. "Because it's us the bear really wants, John. It's you, and me, and Angie he wants. And with the lights on he can see us in here, like mice in a jar." She paused again, and looked at a window.

"And there's really nothing to keep him out." She stared at the window. "Nothing but a thin sheet of glass." She was still staring at the porch window. "If he decided to come in and get us, he'd come right through that window."

Blue-John asked anxiously, "What will we do?"

"Just hope he doesn't decide to come in and get us," answered Mrs. Brinkman quietly. She got the shotgun. "And try to be ready if he does. We'd better keep an eye on him." They stepped cautiously to the window. The bear was still in the yard, pacing between the house and the rabbit hutches. "And hope your dad and Tex Doan get home soon."

Angie came into the kitchen. "Why are the lights out, Mama?"

Mrs. Brinkman looked around. "So the bear will go home. Shh!" She smiled nervously and put her finger to her lips. "We're trying to fool that old bear. Shh!"

"Oh," whispered Angie. "Can you get supper, at the same time you're fooling the bear?"

Blue-John scowled at her and started to say something but suddenly a splintering crash broke the stillness. Blue-John and his mother looked out the window.

The bear was smashing the rabbit hutches. One by one he tore apart the hutches, crushing each rabbit with a quick blow of a massive paw. Roaring with rage, he splintered the cages and smashed the feed cabinet, scattering the feed.

Mrs. Brinkman and Blue-John watched in horror. Angie tried to crowd between them. "Let me see the bear," she pleaded. "What's all the noise?" Mrs. Brinkman gave Blue-John the shotgun, picked up

Angie, and carried her into her room. "Shh," she teased, putting Angie on her bed. "Stay here, Honey, and be quiet." She hurried back to the kitchen.

Burrs was pacing from room to room, growling and bristling angrily. "Burrs, hush!" Mrs. Brinkman commanded sharply.

Blue-John was standing at the window, looking out. Mrs. Brinkman put her arm around his shoulder. "John, you're crying." She hugged him close. "Don't cry, son. The rabbits died instantly. They didn't feel any pain."

"It ain't the rabbits I'm crying about," murmured Blue-John.

"Then what—?" She glanced out the other window and saw headlights coming, far down the lane. "Oh, thank heaven!" she cried, and turned Blue-John to see where she was pointing. "Look, John! It must be Will and Tex coming!"

Suddenly Angie screamed, a thin, piercing scream.

"Angie," gasped Mrs. Brinkman. She snatched the shotgun from Blue-John and dashed out of the kitchen, with Blue-John at her heels. In her room, Angie was huddled against the head of her bed, crying. Mrs. Brinkman laid the shotgun on the bed and took Angie in her arms and comforted her. "What is it, Angie? What is it?"

"The bear," sobbed the child. "Outside my win-

dow. I heard it! Outside my window!" Her tiny voice
rose to a thin wail.

"There, there," comforted her mother. Mrs. Brinkman looked at Blue-John. "He's circling the house."
She gasped and jumped up. "Will and Tex! They
won't see him in the dark!" They bolted from the
room together.

Before they reached the kitchen the porch window
shattered in a shower of broken glass, as the bear,
roaring, plunged his huge head and shoulders into
the kitchen. Popping and snapping his teeth, he
started to squeeze in through the narrow opening.

Mrs. Brinkman screamed. "The shotgun!" She
whirled and ran back to Angie's room. Blue-John
frantically looked around for something to hit the
bear with.

At that instant, in a snarling flash of brown and
white, Burrs streaked into the kitchen and leaped
head on at the raging bear. The little dog grabbed
the bear's cheek. With a roar the bear shook his
head and flipped Burrs into a corner of the kitchen.
Barking fiercely, the tiny dog attacked again, spring-
ing to meet the bear and clamping onto the bear's
nose. With an ear-splitting bellow, the bear abruptly
backed out of the window, with the tiny dog still
clinging to his nose.

They disappeared outside.

Mrs. Brinkman rushed into the kitchen with the shotgun. She saw the bear was gone, and asked, "Where's Burrs?"

"Outside! With the bear!" shouted Blue-John. He leaped to the door. His mother grabbed his arm. "No, John! You're not going out there!" The boy squirmed away and opened the door, just as Tex Doan's truck turned into the driveway.

"Oh, thank heaven, thank heaven!" cried Mrs. Brinkman. She and Blue-John rushed out to the truck. "Will! Will! Oh, Honey, I'm so glad you're home. The bear! He tried to break into the kitchen!"

"What!" shouted Mr. Brinkman, getting out of the truck. His injured foot was wrapped in a bandage and he used two crutches to walk. "Where is the bear now?"

Tex Doan came around the truck. "Hi, Chris," he said.

"Hi, Tex. I don't know where the bear is now, Will. Gone, I guess. Burrs chased him away, I guess."

"Burrs! That little mutt? Chased away that bear?" Mr. Brinkman shook his head. "Well, are you and the kids all right?"

Mrs. Brinkman leaned against him, crying a little. "We're all right. We're all right." They started toward the house. "The rabbits are all dead. The bear smashed the hutches. And the kitchen window is broken out, and the cabbages—"

"It had to happen," interrupted Mr. Brinkman. "Well, I'm in no shape to hunt down that brute. Maybe we'll have to . . ." He glanced toward the barn. "Are the cows okay? Too bad about Molly's calf." He looked again. "Say, it looks like the barn door wasn't latched, or something."

Blue-John looked. Something about the barn door wasn't right, but in the slanting light of the yard floodlight it was hard to see it clearly. "I thought I closed and latched it, when I milked the cows," he said, puzzled. "I'll go close it."

"Oh, go on in with your mother, John," directed Mr. Brinkman. "The cows are probably nervous from the bear's attack. I'll try to quiet them down, and close the door, too. Be back in a minute, Christine, and Tex and me will do something about that window."

"Okay, Honey, I'll heat up the coffee."

"And I'll just take a stroll around the house," suggested Tex Doan, "just to make sure that bear has lit out. Got a flashlight in the house, Chris?"

"Uh, sure," answered Mrs. Brinkman, absently. "It's strange, John, but I thought you had latched that barn door, too." They went toward the house and Mr. Brinkman bobbed toward the barn, swinging on the crutches. By the time he reached the barn Tex Doan stepped out of the house with the flashlight.

"Hey!" called Mr. Brinkman. "This door's broken!"

"Broken?" replied Tex Doan.

"Hanging on one hinge. Ask Blue-John what happened to it. Did he run the tractor into it?" He awkwardly pulled the door open and went inside.

Tex stuck his head into the kitchen and spoke to Blue-John, who was sweeping up broken window glass. "Hey, High-pockets, did y'all run the tractor into the barn door? Your daddy says it's hanging on one hinge." He grinned, but when he saw the expression on Blue-John's face he stopped grinning. He looked at Mrs. Brinkman.

Mrs. Brinkman put her hand to her mouth. "The bear! The bear's in there!" Tex Doan whirled and leaped from the porch in one step and raced for the barn with Blue-John right behind him.

Suddenly a savage roar shook the barn. Snarling and bellowing in rage, the bear had something, or someone, trapped.

Blue-John and Tex ran into the barn and stared in horror.

Molly was down, lying in a far corner of the barn. She was bleeding.

Mr. Brinkman was backed into a corner in Molly's stall. He was down, under Molly's hayrack. Because the hayrack slanted out over his head he could not climb out of the stall on that side, and the bear, pacing and raging back and forth in front of him, wouldn't let him crawl across the stall and get out on the other side. He was poking the crutch at the bear.

Cowering in the opposite corner was the white rooster, also trapped.

Roaring and snarling, the great bear raged, swinging his head and snapping his jaws. Saliva foamed from his mouth and his hair stood up in a bristly ruff over his huge shoulders.

In the next stall Ginger was in panic. She was leaping and threshing in her stall, in a frenzy to escape the bear. She was slamming into the walls of her stall, and bawling in terror. The boards of her stall were cracking and splintering under the impact.

Without a word between them Blue-John and Tex Doan whirled and raced from the barn. Tex Doan ran toward his truck, and Blue-John dashed toward the tractor shed.

Blue-John raced into the shed and whirled around, frantically searching the walls in the dim light of the yard floodlight. Then he saw what he was looking for and leaped up on the tool bench. With one sweep of his arm he cleared the cans of paint and nails from the shelf.

There was the rifle!

He snatched it up, leaped from the tool bench, and ran for the barn. As he ran he frantically jerked back the bolt to load the rifle. A brass cartridge spun out of the rifle. Blue-John looked back in dismay. One shot lost! He had misunderstood! He hadn't realized the chamber in the rifle had been loaded. He looked down into the magazine and saw more cartridges.

He slammed shut the bolt as he ran into the barn.

The bear seemed closer to his stepfather, but still it had not attacked. The roaring and bellowing of the bear seemed to shake the walls of the barn.

Blue-John raised the rifle. It was too long and heavy for him to aim carefully, so he lifted it as high as he could, and pointed it at the bear.

The bear suddenly stood up on his hind legs, massive and gigantic in the little stall, and moved toward the trapped man. At that instant the rooster panicked. In a burst of white feathers he leaped up and tried to fly out of the stall. He was fat and heavy, however, and he bumped the bear as he flapped past. The bear, distracted, whirled and swung at the rooster.

He missed, but for an instant he was drawn away from the man in the corner, and loomed over Blue-John, standing in the doorway.

In that instant Blue-John pulled the trigger.

The thunderous roar of the rifle drowned out all other sounds.

Blue-John staggered back and almost fell.

With a bawl of pain the bear spun around and fell. He was on his feet instantly, raging and snapping at the wound in his great body.

Blue-John jerked back the bolt and the empty shell spun out. He slammed the bolt shut, pointed the rifle, and again pulled the trigger.

The rifle thundered again, and again he staggered back.

The bear fell again, bellowing and raging in pain and defiance. Blood foamed from his mouth. He staggered to his feet, glaring at Blue-John.

Another rifle thundered beside Blue-John. Tex Doan was there, but Blue-John didn't look. His eyes were filling with tears. The empty shell was a yellow blur as he jacked it out of the rifle. He looked at the great bear. It was down, and dying, but dying hard, roaring defiance to the end.

"I'm jammed, John," yelled Tex Doan. "You'll have to finish it." He was struggling to unjam his rifle. "You'll have to finish it!"

Blue-John lifted the rifle. His arms seemed to have no feeling. Everything was blurred. Tex Doan's voice seemed a long way off. Blue-John stared at the bear. He could see it, dimly, in a mist of rainy light, through the tears.

He felt the bear was looking at him, with its dying eyes.

He pulled the trigger.

The rifle thundered and he fell back.

Slowly he lowered the rifle and slumped to the ground. For a brief moment he stared at the awesome scene in Molly's stall. The air was filled with dust and bits of chaff, making the light hazy. His stepfather crouched in the corner, grimly gripping his crutch. Tex Doan stood beside him. Out of the corner of his eye Blue-John dimly saw his mother behind them, with the shotgun.

The king bear lay still and quiet, a massive, rounded mound of bristly brown fur on the barn floor. The great cables of muscles were relaxed, torn and channeled by rifle bullets. The fearless heart was shattered, blown to pulp by the bullets. The broad head rested on a limp paw, the eyes now dull and unseeing.

Fine gray dust slowly settled on the old bear.

Blue-John cried softly, "I told you to go away. Why didn't you just go away?"

He got up and hurried to help his stepfather.

CHAPTER ELEVEN

A Clicking, Clinking, Clanking

THE sun burned warm and golden in a cloud-less sky of crystal blue over the Brinkman home-stead the next morning. Still damp from the rain, willows and alders glistened in the sunlight. A single moose wandered across the long north meadow as six plump spruce hens rocketed overhead and disappeared into the shadows of the woods.

In the hayloft of the Brinkman barn the mice were squeaking in the oat bundles. Below, Molly was back in her stall. She lay quietly, weak and nervous. There were four deep gashes across the ribs of her left side. The raw gashes had been washed out and thickly smeared with a disinfectant salve. Ginger slowly paced her stall. The scent of the bear still hung heavy in the barn.

A wide, shallow groove in the chaff on the barn floor led from Molly's stall out through the big front door.

Outside, at the end of the groove, lay the bear.

At the house a big piece of cardboard covered the porch window. In the kitchen, Burrs was stretched out on an old plaid shirt near the kitchen stove. He was unmarked except for a swollen left eye, and he staggered when he tried to walk. He was recovering from a concussion he suffered when the bear threw him against the light pole in the yard. Mrs. Brinkman had found him there, unconscious, last night.

Mr. and Mrs. Brinkman and Angie were ready to eat breakfast. It was unusually quiet in the kitchen. Mrs. Brinkman put a platter of fried eggs and moose sausage on the table and sat down.

"Where's John?" asked Angie.

"He'll be here in a minute," replied Mrs. Brinkman quietly. They began to eat breakfast. They ate in silence. Mrs. Brinkman glanced occasionally toward the living room to see if Blue-John was coming.

"What about the bear, Daddy?" asked Angie. "Are you going to make the bear into a rug? He sure is big and scratchy-looking." She didn't eat; she just sat there, chattering. "He tried to come in our house, Daddy. He tried to come right in *here*!" she exclaimed, waving at the shattered window. "And he

165

mashed our rabbits." She lowered her voice. "Our poor little rabbits are all mashed to pieces, Daddy. Daddy, will we eat the rabbits? Daddy—"

"Hush, Angie," Mrs. Brinkman interrupted. Blue-John could be heard coming to the kitchen. He came in slowly and sat down. His eyes were puffy. Angie stole a glance at him, and then at her parents. They all ate in silence.

Finally Mr. Brinkman spoke. "John, I'm—sorry it turned out this way," he said gently. "We all are."

After a moment Blue-John answered. "Sure, Dad, I know." He ate without looking up. "It just—happened. I guess I knew it would."

"A grizzly bear is an hombre and a loner, John," said Mr. Brinkman quietly. "You can't make a pet out of a grizzly. He has too much pride to be someone's pet. And he doesn't want to be crowded. He figures what's his is his, and if he has to fight for it, he'll die the way he lived, afraid of nothing. Anything less, and he wouldn't be a grizzly."

After a moment he continued. "Time had run out on this old bear. We had to crowd him. We had to bury his moose. We live here."

Outside, near the barn, the big white rooster crowed, strutting stiff-legged past the cold body of the old bear. In the corner of the kitchen Burrs moaned softly in his sleep.

"What I can't figure," Mr. Brinkman went on, "is why the bear stopped here in the first place. Why didn't he just keep going?"

The kitchen was silent as they ate, except for the flat clinking of the table service. Finally Angie broke the silence. "Daddy, will we—?"

Her father interrupted. "When my foot is all better I'll build some new hutches and we'll get some new rabbits." He frowned at Angie and she smiled, satisfied.

When they finished breakfast Mr. Brinkman cleared his throat. "Uh, John, when Tex Doan gets here with his dozer he'll scoop out a hole and bury the bear." He paused. "I don't guess you want the hide tanned."

Blue-John shook his head.

"Well—have you got any ideas about—where to bury him?" Blue-John got up and walked into the living room, and then came back.

"How about the end of the potato patch, near the woods?" suggested Blue-John. "Ground is soft there, and there's no stumps."

"Okay, John," answered Mr. Brinkman. "That sounds like a good place." Mrs. Brinkman poured two cups of coffee. She looked out the unbroken upper half of the porch window.

"Tex is coming," she said, getting another cup.

"Dad," began Blue-John.

"Yes."

"Just one thing. It probably sounds kind of silly—but," he hesitated, looking at his mother and stepfather. "Do you have to drag him out there?"

Mr. and Mrs. Brinkman looked at each other, and at Blue-John.

"Why, uh—" Mr. Brinkman hesitated. "As a matter of fact, I'd thought—maybe we could hoist him into the truck with the rope and pulley hanging on the barn. I'm sorry we had to drag him out last night with Tex's truck, but we had to get Molly back in her stall. And Ginger would have been raving mad by morning if we'd left the bear there."

"Yes, sure, I understand," muttered Blue-John. He turned and went to his room. Tex Doan turned his bulldozer into the driveway and clanked to a stop at the kitchen. He got down, leaving the engine running.

"Hi, y'all," he greeted as he came into the kitchen, and hung his cowboy hat on a rack. He scooped up Angie and hugged her.

"Hi, Tex," replied Mr. Brinkman. "Sit down and have some coffee."

" 'Lo, Tex," smiled Mrs. Brinkman. She poured another cup of coffee and began washing the breakfast dishes. "Why don't you run play for a while,

Angie. As soon as the men leave you can help me wash clothes."

"I'll go look at the bear," replied Angie. "Is he dead, Mama?"

"He's dead, Angie."

Angie looked at her mother in surprise. "Aren't you glad?"

"Why, of course, Punkin."

"But you don't sound very glad."

"Never mind. Run and play."

Angie went out, muttering, "Well, *I'm* glad!"

"How's that boy of yours?" asked Tex Doan. "Does he feel more like looking at the world this morning?"

Mr. Brinkman leaned back and stretched out his injured foot. "He's better. Not good, just better. He understands. In fact, maybe he understands too well."

"What do you mean?" asked Tex Doan.

Mrs. Brinkman broke in. "Will means, when people come in, bears have to go."

"This is what John understands, and this is what hurts him," continued Mr. Brinkman.

"Well, that boy might be tenderhearted, but he sure has grit. He beat me to the bear by four steps and just stood there toe to toe and turned it ever' way but loose. He's a young'un to be proud of."

"We are," declared Mr. Brinkman.

"More coffee, Tex?" interrupted Mrs. Brinkman.

"I'd take it kindly, Chris," answered Tex.

"Say, Tex," said Mr. Brinkman, "I got an idea. Let's just haul the bear in the back of my pickup, when we go to bury it."

Tex Doan looked sideways at Mr. Brinkman. "But—"

"And I thought maybe we could bury it at the end of the potato patch, near the woods," Mr. Brinkman continued. He made circles on the table with the coffee cup. "The ground is soft there, and there's no stumps."

Mrs. Brinkman looked at her husband, and smiled a faint smile.

Tex Doan studied Mr. Brinkman for a moment. Then he grinned. "Sure," he said, finishing his coffee. "I'm ready when you are." They got up. "Of course," grinned Tex Doan to Mr. Brinkman, "you ain't going to be much help, walking on them sticks." He nodded at Mr. Brinkman's crutches.

"I'll supervise," grinned Mr. Brinkman. He turned to his wife. "I'm not kidding, Chris. I can't drive the truck, or even pull the rope. We'll need your help, Honey."

"Oh, no, Will," said Mrs. Brinkman. She looked at her husband. "Well, I guess I could. It hadn't occurred to me that you couldn't help. Well, someone

170

has to do it." She turned back to the sink. "Just let me finish these dishes."

Blue-John appeared in the doorway. "I'll drive, Dad."

They all looked in surprise at him. "Oh, that's all right, John. I'll do it," offered his mother. "With Tex's dozer it won't take long."

"I'd really like to, Mom." Blue-John's voice was flat and dull. "I like to drive the truck. Okay, Dad?"

"Sure, John. We need a good hand to help. Come on." Mr. Brinkman hobbled out as Tex Doan held open the door. Blue-John followed. Mrs. Brinkman shook her head, looking after Blue-John.

They went out to the barn. They hoisted the body of the old bear into the back of the truck. Mr. Brinkman and Angie got into the cab of the truck. Blue-John started around the truck, then checked himself. He stepped back and stared at one of the bear's front legs that was sticking up above the tail gate. He looked closer. It was a left leg. There was blood on it, and yellow dust. Gently he ruffled the hair on the back of the foot, and saw what he was looking for.

"Want one of them claws, for a souvenir?" called Tex Doan from the waiting dozer.

Startled, Blue-John turned, then shook his head. He ran to get into the truck.

They drove out to the potato patch, with the truck leading. Blue-John, Mr. Brinkman, and Angie rode in silence in front. The bear was a brown lump of old fur in back. One foreleg, matted with blood, stuck out stiffly over the tail gate. The sun glinted dully on the heavy claws, and on the small patches of dead white hair almost hidden under the blood, and on the yellow dust.

At the end of the potato patch Blue-John stopped. Mr. Brinkman and Angie got out and watched Tex Doan scoop out a huge hole with the dozer. With a chain Tex Doan pulled the bear's body out of the truck, into the hole. Blue-John pulled the truck out of the way.

He sat in the cab of the truck, staring silently into the woods, as Tex Doan's dozer surged back and forth, shoving the brown clay soil into the hole, covering the soft brown fur, the massive shoulders, the broad head, the terrible claws, quickly, efficiently. The snarl of the dozer echoed off the trees where the bear had prowled, and surged in waves across the hayfield where he had run down the moose, and bounced off the barn where he had boldly stolen the calf and, finally, went down under the roaring guns.

Tex Doan worked the snarling, clicking, clanking

bulldozer back and forth across the grave, packing down the earth into a smooth, brown mound.

It was done.

A raven watched curiously from a bare, dead tree.

Mr. Brinkman and Angie got into the pickup and Blue-John drove back to the house. Blue-John and Angie went inside. Mr. Brinkman waited at the truck for Tex Doan.

In the kitchen, Mrs. Brinkman had pulled the washing machine near the sink. It made a churning, sloshing sound, as she filled the rinse tubs with buckets of water from the well.

Angie got a carrot from the refrigerator, and Blue-John went directly to his room.

"Well, we buried that old bear, Mama." Angie munched the carrot. "Tex Doan made a big hole in the ground and put the bear in it and covered it all up with dirt. Mama, the bear is really dead now, ain't it?"

Mrs. Brinkman had watched Blue-John come in and silently go to his room. "The bear is all dead, Angie," she answered absently.

"And he won't kill no more rabbits," muttered Angie, positively. Mrs. Brinkman went on filling the rinse tubs with water.

In a moment there was the sound of the front

door opening, and after a pause, it closed. Mrs. Brinkman was puzzled. They seldom used the front door. She went into the living room and looked out.

Blue-John was walking through the front yard of clover and wild grass. He was carrying a cage. When he reached the row of elderberry and alder bushes at the edge of the yard he put down the cage and opened it. He tapped it and shook it gently and the meadow mice scurried out. He brought the cage back and left it outside the house.

When he came into the living room he saw his mother and smiled. She smiled and said, "I'll hold open the door, if you like."

"Okay, thanks," replied Blue-John. He went into his room and came out with the squirrel cage. Mrs. Brinkman opened the door for him.

This time he went through the elderberries and into the woods beyond. The squirrel darted up a tree when it was released.

Angie had come into the living room and was watching Blue-John. "Mama, what is John doing?"

"He's letting his pets go," answered Mrs. Brinkman.

"Why is he doing that? Don't he like them no more?"

"Of course he does, Sweetie. It's just that—well, it's hard to explain."

Blue-John left the cage outside and went into his room once more. He took the third cage deep into the woods, where the little owl would find darker shadows in which to wait out the daylight hours. When he came back in he silently gathered together the food supplies he had kept in his room for the animals. As he came out of his room Angie asked, "Why did you let the animals go, John?"

Blue-John looked at Angie, and then at his mother. He shrugged. "I don't know. Just felt like it, I guess." He went on out through the kitchen. The screen door banged.

Mr. Brinkman and Tex Doan were standing at the bulldozer, talking. They had watched Blue-John release his animals, and now watched him scatter the leftover oats and cornflakes to the chickens. He went around to the front of the house and got the cages, and carried them to the tractor shed.

They stared in astonishment as he then went to the lean-to that leaned against the barn, poked around inside, and came out with a hoe. He balanced the hoe on his shoulder and started toward the garden.

He was halfway to the garden before Mr. Brinkman got over his astonishment and yelled, "Hey, John! You're not going to chop weeds, are you?"

Blue-John stopped and turned around. His voice

drifted back. "Naw. I—I was just going to do something about these cabbages. They got all busted up by . . ." His voice faded out.

"Seems like a tomfool thing to do," bellowed Tex Doan, "seeing as how I wanted you to help me fly your daddy over to Seward. Got to get him back in the hospital."

Blue-John stood looking at the men for a moment. Slowly he started walking back. Suddenly he began running. As he passed the lean-to he threw the hoe like a spear.

It sailed through the doorway and clattered and banged inside.